MY DEMON IS A DARLING

MY DEMON IS A DARLING

IGRAINE I O GRAY

First published in 2024
by Unconventional Heretics Press
Vauxhall Bridge Road,
London
SW1V 2SA

Copyright © Igraine Gray, 2024

Igraine Gray has asserted her right under the Copyright, Designs and Patents Act, 1988, to be identified as Author of this work.

All rights reserved. No part of this book publication may be reproduced or transmitted in any form or by any means, electronic or mechanical, including photocopying, recording, or any information storage or retrieval system, without prior permission in writing from the publishers.

A catalogue record for this book is available from the British Library.

ISBN: 978-1-7390897-2-6

For all those who found home a little later in life, and to those who helped them find it.

CONTENT GUIDANCE

This novel explores aspects of distressing human experience, and contains references to grief, sexual assault, and suicide. Please read with care.

CHAPTER 1

Some New Fields, Baba

Humanity was the death of joy. Of that much I was certain. Way too conscious, craving more life, and the cycle would never cease. In my mind, their story was the beginning of the end or the end of the beginning, and I did not have the fortitude to pick a side. Simply, pain will out.

Perched atop the cold, moss-covered tombstone, I observed the sombre spectacle of a funeral unfolding before me with a morbid fascination. The mourners, clad in sombre black, their faces a kaleidoscope of grief, revealed the depths of human emotion that only Death could unearth. Some wept openly, their sobs echoing like the cries of lost souls, as others stood stony-eyed, their hearts frozen by the icy grip of grief. The inconsolable wails of the bereaved rent the very fabric of the air itself, as they consoled one another with embraces that did nothing to chase away the frigid embrace of the Reaper.

My saurian eyes followed the polished casket, adorned with fragrant blooms, as it descended into the gaping maw of the Earth, a final voyage for the departed. The priest's sonorous voice, imbued with the authority of age-old prayers, drifted on the wind like whispers from beyond the veil, beseeching the Almighty for mercy and solace. Yet, I knew all too well that the only human responses he would receive were the muffled echoes of his own desires, bouncing off the cold, indifferent stars.

As the mourners dispersed, the floral tributes wilted, and the priest's words were carried away like the autumn leaves, the harsh truth remained: life was transient, a fleeting illusion that danced upon the stage of existence, destined to be extinguished without so much as a whimper. In the grand scheme of things, the petty dramas and conflicts that consumed mortal lives seemed as fleeting as the sparks from a firefly's tail.

Yet, in this dance of futility, I found a perverse beauty, a reminder that each heartbeat, each breath, was a stolen moment from the jaws of Oblivion. My flickering tongue tasted the salty tang of human grief, imbued with the bittersweet nectar of their fleeting existence. How tragic, I mused, that it took the cold embrace of Death to awaken them from their slumber of complacency.

I jumped up, the soil shaking, and committed to leaving behind the mortal realm to its daily machinations. In the distance, the first light of dawn crept over the horizon, kindling the stars to extinguish their dying flames, ushering in a new day, and the endless cycle of life and death continued, unabated, unyielding, and ever-changing.

In the cold, unforgiving expanse of home, I smiled, knowing that I would be there, ever-vigilant, ever-present, to bear witness to their short, brilliant lives, and to be the one constant in their endless dance with the void.

I pondered, "What would you do if you knew that tomorrow was not promised?" For in the end, I surmised, it was not the quantity of days, but the quality of life that left an ineffaceable mark upon the sands of time. Little did I know that I would soon be a party to one of many such stories on the matter.

For it was at this funeral, that I first encountered one half of this indelible tale. A widower of no and yet much import, there seemed not anything to distinguish him from the rest. And yet now I know, it was all to come.

The celestial firmament above me seemed to nod in agreement, the sun's fiery chariot ascending in a blaze of crimson and gold, illuminating the unknown path that lay ahead for those who still walked the earthly realm. I, for my part, would continue my eternal vigil, a silent sentinel to their hopes, their dreams, and their fears, a reminder that even in the darkest night, there is always a flicker of light, waiting to be kindled.

In the vast, indifferent cosmos, I found solace in the knowledge that I had made a difference, no matter how small, in the lives of those I had encountered. And as the winds of Fate conspired to weave their intricate tapestry, I knew that my journey, much like the one I am about to tell, was far from over.

So, the cycle of life, death, and rebirth continued its relentless march, a perpetual ballet set to the rhythm of the beating heart of the universe. The characters would change, and the setting might shift, but the story remained the same.

And who am I you might ask? Well that is an excellent question, though I am sure no introduction should be required. You know me as well as they did.

I will always be waiting.

In the shadows, watching.

Until the end of time itself. Because that is how long this story remains.

CHAPTER 2

New Place, Same Road, That's Life

Narrator's Note 14.36.4.2 - When looking for ghosts, it is probably wise to acquire a haunted house.

With a heavy sigh, Vivienne descended from the bus and her tattered shoes scraped against the cracked pavement of Skinningrove village. The once sturdy soles were now worn thin from endless miles of walking, offering little protection from the rough terrain. Each step sent jolts of pain up her legs, a constant reminder of the harsh reality she was facing. She gazed wearily at the desolate streets, lined with rows of dreary street houses and quaint stone cottages that seemed to blend into the grey sky above. It was a stark contrast to the bustling city she had left behind. The silence enveloped her like a thick fog, broken only by the distant cry of seagulls and the occasional rustle of leaves in the wind.

The village appeared trapped in perpetual slumber, as if time had stopped ticking forward. A thick, eerie stillness clung to the air, broken only by the faint crashing of waves against the shore in the distance. Vivienne huddled deeper into her threadbare coat, attempting to shield herself from the sharp, biting wind that carried the unmistakable scent of salt and decaying wood. The abandoned buildings loomed over her like forgotten giants, their windows shattered and doors hanging on rusty hinges. It was a haunting scene, one that seemed frozen in time and devoid of any signs of life. But for Vivienne, it was all too familiar - a place she once called home, now a desolate wasteland consumed by nature's grip.

"Is this really the right place?" she whispered to herself, her voice barely audible above the rustling of the leaves. Doubt crept into her mind, mingling with the desperation that had driven her to this forgotten corner of the world. She had heard whispers of the haunted cottage by the sea, a place where the lost and the broken could find solace. But now, standing alone in the empty streets, Vivienne questioned the wisdom of her decision.

A rusted, weather-worn signpost creaked in the salty breeze. Vivienne followed the faded arrow, her heart racing with equal parts excitement and fear. She gingerly placed one foot in front of the other, careful not to trip on the overgrown path. The earth below was soft and uneven, reclaimed by tangled weeds and vibrant wildflowers. Her petite frame strained with each step, weakened by years of malnutrition and neglect.

Each step she took on the deserted street was accompanied by a sharp, stinging memory. The images replayed in her mind like a broken record - his lies, her trust shattered, and the gaping emptiness that now filled her life. She clenched her fists, willing herself to keep moving forward, but the pain threatened to overwhelm her with each passing moment. Vivienne's heart felt as though it had been sliced open by shards of glass, and she couldn't escape the agony of betrayal, violation, and loss that consumed her thoughts.

Despite her trembling voice, she spoke with fierce determination. "You're stronger than this," she whispered, the words carrying a weight of hope and desperation. Memories of past struggles flooded her mind as she tried to convince herself of their truth. But deep down, doubt still lingered like a dark cloud, threatening to consume her fragile resolve.

As she trudged through the thick mist, Vivienne's heart pounded with a mixture of fear and anticipation. The cottage loomed closer, its decrepit form revealing itself like a haunting spectre emerging from the darkness. The crooked walls and sagging roof seemed to whisper of a past filled with untold sorrows and dark secrets. As she reached the threshold, her breath caught in her throat, knowing that this was the beginning of her new life, one full of unknown dangers and possibilities.

Vivienne's hand shook as she approached the quaint cottage. She hesitated before reaching for the brass doorknob, knowing that behind it lay a path filled with obstacles and struggles. But the thought of having a safe haven and an opportunity to start anew gave her the courage to take one small step at a time toward the unknown.

The old, worn door groaned in protest as Vivienne pushed it open, its hinges creaking like a chorus of rusty violins. The eerie sound echoed through the abandoned cottage, causing chills to run down her spine. Stepping delicately across the threshold, her footfalls stirred up clouds of dust that danced in the faint light filtering through the grimy windows. The once beautiful room was now covered in layers of neglect and decay, like a forgotten memory. But despite its dilapidated state, there was still a lingering sense of mystery and longing within its walls.

As Vivienne's eyes adjusted to the gloom, she took in the space before her. A place that was once a home, now reduced to a mere shell of its former self. The walls were adorned with faded and peeling wallpaper, remnants of happier times that now told a sombre tale. She could hear the floorboards creaking beneath her feet, burdened by the weight of countless untold stories. Each step revealed another layer of history, each creak a memory waiting to be discovered.

The dilapidated house was small and sparse, with peeling paint and threadbare carpet. Looking around, the reality of how far she had fallen hit her hard. She whispered to herself,

"It's not much, but it's mine" tracing her fingers along the frayed edges of a worn sofa. The bitterness in her voice reflected the desperation she felt at this moment.

With each step, Vivienne delved further into the forgotten cottage, her eyes taking in the remnants of a life long since passed. The tattered curtain, once adorned with vibrant colours and intricate patterns, now hung limply in the draft, its beauty faded by time and dirt. A photograph, its edges curled and its surface yellowed, clung stubbornly to the peeling wallpaper. The faces of its subjects were obscured by a thick veil of grime, their identities lost to the ravages of time. As she moved deeper into the cottage, it was as if she was unravelling a forgotten story, piece by piece, until all that remained were fragments of a distant past.

"I wonder what stories these walls would tell if they could speak," Vivienne mused, her fingertips grazing the rough surface of the wood. The cottage seemed to hold its secrets close, a silent guardian of the unseen.

Vivienne cautiously made her way through the debris and ruins of what used to be a home. Each step was muffled by layers of dust, sending small clouds swirling into the air. The dim light that filtered in through boarded-up windows highlighted the peeling wallpaper and cracked floors, giving the space an eerie glow. But amidst the desolation, she couldn't help but feel a spark of excitement. This abandoned house held secrets and endless possibilities, a chance for her to leave her tumultuous past behind and create a new future. She could almost hear the walls whispering stories of its former inhabitants, urging her to uncover their mysteries. And as she stood in it all, Vivienne couldn't help but feel like she was on the brink of something extraordinary.

Vivienne took a deep, fortifying breath and forced her gaze away from the peeling wallpaper that seemed to mock her with its decay. The faded patterns were a stark contrast to the rest of the room, which was in disarray. Clothes were scattered on the floor, books haphazardly stacked on shelves, and dishes piled up in the sink. But instead of succumbing to the memories that threatened to consume her, Vivienne focused on the task at hand. She knew that dwelling on the past would only serve to drag her down into the abyss of despair. With determination in her heart and a sense of purpose, she channelled her energy into bringing order to the chaos that surrounded her. Each item she put away or cleaned was a small victory over the overwhelming darkness that had taken hold of her home.

Vivienne's stomach rumbled loudly, a constant reminder of her hunger. But she refused to let it distract her from the task at hand. She rolled up her sleeves, revealing faded scars that marred her arms. Each one was a symbol of the hardships she had faced and overcome. As she approached the cottage's windows, their glass panes coated in grime and layers of dirt, she felt a familiar determination take hold.

With relentless strokes, she scrubbed away at the filth, letting in streams of sunlight that cascaded into the once-dark and dreary space. The beams of light danced across the room, highlighting the worn but sturdy furniture and peeling wallpaper. Vivienne couldn't help but draw parallels between herself and the neglected cottage. Both had been battered and beaten by life, but both still held the potential for beauty and restoration.

As she continued to clean, Vivienne's mind wandered to her own journey of healing and resilience. Just like she was bringing light back into the forgotten corners of the cottage, she knew she could also rise from the ashes of her past and find new purpose and strength within herself. And as she stood in the now bright and inviting space, she felt a sense of hope wash over her – a promise of brighter days ahead.

"One step at a time," Vivienne muttered under her breath, her brow furrowed in concentration as she tackled the debris that littered the floor. Each sweep of the broom, each discarded remnant of the past, brought her closer.

With a worn rag clutched tightly in one hand and a bucket of soapy water balanced precariously in the other, Vivienne scrubbed fiercely at the dirt-caked windows. The grime had accumulated over the years, stubbornly clinging to the glass in layers upon layers. As she worked, her mind drifted to the blank canvas waiting for her in the corner of the room, beckoning her with its promise of creativity and escape from the monotonous task. But as the sun began to set, casting an amber glow through the streaks on the window, Vivienne's weariness became all-consuming. Every muscle in her body ached and even her heavy eyelids seemed to weigh her down. The once-daunting task of cleaning now felt like an impossible challenge, draining her both physically and mentally. She longed for the refreshing coolness of a shower and the comforting embrace of her bed, but she knew she couldn't stop until every last bit of grime was banished from those windows.

With a weary sigh, she set the broom aside and reached for a tattered candle, its wick yearning for the kiss of a flame. With the strike of a match and the smell of heat, the candle sputtered to life, casting an eerie dance of light and shadow across the room.

Vivienne sank into the worn embrace of the couch, the ancient springs creaking beneath her weight. As she settled into the musty cushions, she allowed her eyelids to flutter shut, the flickering candlelight painting abstract shapes against her closed lids.

The soft glow of the dwindling candle cast dancing shadows on the walls, stretching and elongating them until they seemed to take on a life of their own. Vivienne's body was heavy with fatigue, and she could feel the weight of her struggles weighing her down. But as the night wore on and the darkness deepened, she allowed herself to surrender to its embrace, finding solace in the peaceful respite it offered. Tomorrow would surely bring new challenges, but for now, she would let herself be consumed by the quiet stillness of this moment, trusting that even the longest of nights must eventually give way to the promise of a new day.

With a trembling hand, Vivienne reached into the depths of her weathered, old patchwork bag, all frayed at the seams, colours muted. A bag her grandmother had gifted her when she was ten. Within, her fingers brushed the familiar contours of her salvaged treasures: a sketchbook – its pages stained with struggles past – and pencils, nubs of graphite. She drew it forth, along with a handful of worn pencils, their once-sharp points dulled by countless hours of use. She stood up quickly, her body surprised at the sudden movement, moving over to the rocking chair in the corner, whose music had not stopped at all, its creaking narrating her evening from the moment she had stepped foot in there.

Vivienne sat cross-legged on the threadbare rug, her sketchbook resting in her lap. She took a moment to breathe in the familiar smell of old books and dust that filled the cottage. Her pencil hovered over the blank page before her, eager to bring the abandoned house to life. With a firm grip, she began to draw, her hand moving swiftly and confidently across the paper. As lines formed and shapes emerged, she captured every detail of the crumbling windows, the peeling paint, and the sagging roof with precision and grace. The cottage came alive on the page, just as it had in Vivienne's mind.

As she sketched, Vivienne felt a sense of purpose suffuse her weary bones.

"You've always had a gift," a voice whispered in her mind, a ghostly echo of her grandmother. Vivienne's lips curved into a faint smile, begrudgingly acknowledging the truth of those words. And now, as she sat in the fading candlelight, her pencil dancing across the page, Vivienne felt a contentment, an easiness within her chest.

As the night wore on, Vivienne's eyelids grew heavy, the weight of exhaustion pressing down upon her like a leaden blanket. She set aside her sketchbook, the pages now filled with intricate renderings of the cottage's haunting beauty, and stretched out upon the worn couch, her body sinking into the threadbare cushions.

The moonlight seeped through the shattered windows, illuminating the cottage in an otherworldly glow. Vivienne's heart pounded as she watched the building come to life before her eyes. It seemed to breathe and pulsate with a sinister energy that both thrilled and terrified her to her core.

"You're not alone," a voice seemed to whisper in the stillness, a gentle caress against her troubled mind.

Vivienne closed her eyes, letting the soothing words wash over her like a balm. For the first time in years, she felt a glimmer of hope, a sense that perhaps, just perhaps, she could rise above the pain and trauma that had defined her existence for so long.

Vivienne slumped back in her chair, her heart racing as she squeezed her eyes shut. The voice seemed to coil around her like a python, its venomous words sinking into her skin and seeping through her veins. A wave of intense heat enveloped Vivienne's body, making her feel like she was suffocating in a blanket of fire. But amidst the pain, a spark of hope ignited within her chest, daring to believe that there might still be a way out of the endless darkness that had consumed her for so long.

The moon illuminated her sleeping form, and as she fidgeted, Vivienne knew she had finally found a place to call home, a cure or a curse.

CHAPTER 3

Sally's Not Waiting Any Longer

Narrator's Note 24.23.2.1 and 24.1.1.1 - Objects in windows may appear more stable than they are in actuality.

Vivienne fought with all her might to force open the old wooden door again, her muscles straining and trembling under the weight. With a loud, agonising screech, the rusted hinges finally gave way, sending shivers down her spine. As she cautiously stepped inside, her heavy boots left deep imprints on the dusty floorboards, each creak and groan echoing through the vast empty space. The overpowering stench of decay assaulted her senses, suffocating her as she scanned the desolate room illuminated by only slivers of light peeking through the filthy windows. Shadows lurked in every corner, dancing menacingly along the peeling wallpaper and decaying furniture. The only sounds were the skittering of rodents and the haunting hoots of an owl outside, adding to the eerie atmosphere that surrounded her.

Vivienne's sharp gaze swept over the dilapidated wallpaper, its once bold and intricate designs now faded and obscured by layers of thick dust and tangled cobwebs. Despite her tireless efforts to scrub it clean the night before, the relentless march of time had taken its toll, leaving behind a sickly, muted palette. As she tentatively reached out to trace the rough surface with her trembling fingers, a sudden chill ran down her spine. It was as if the old cottage itself was whispering to her, urging her to unravel its secrets and uncover its hidden past. Every nook and cranny seemed to hold a story, waiting to be heard and understood.

Her hand shook uncontrollably as she traced the peeling wallpaper, feeling the sharp edges of splintered wood and flaking paint against her skin. "This is home now," she croaked, her voice barely audible over the thunderous pounding of her heart. The room was a sanctuary unlike any she had known before, with its soft bed and warm walls that enveloped her in a cocoon of safety. After years of sleeping on cold concrete and makeshift beds of cardboard, the simple luxury of a roof over her head felt like an impossible dream. A sense of disbelief overwhelmed her as she realised she finally had a place to call her own, a refuge from the unforgiving streets that had been her only home for far too long.

Vivienne moved towards the small bedroom, her few belongings clutched tightly to her chest like a lifeline. The room was sparse, a single bed pushed against the wall, its mattress thin and lumpy. A battered dresser stood in the corner, its drawers hanging crookedly, as if even the furniture had given up on any semblance of order.

With a sigh, she unpacked, carefully placing her meagre possessions on the dresser's dusty surface. A worn photograph of a smiling couple, their faces faded and creased, a reminder of a past she could barely remember. A tattered journal, its pages filled with the scribbled musings of a troubled mind. A small wooden box, its contents a mystery even to her.

With trembling hands, she smoothed out the wrinkled bed sheets and placed her few belongings on the nightstand. The small cottage, with its peeling paint and creaky floorboards, was her sanctuary now, a haven from years of wandering without purpose. But as she settled into her new home, a mix of emotions flooded her chest - relief at finally having a place to call her own, yet anxious about what the future held. She took a deep breath, trying to shake off the weight of uncertainty that threatened to suffocate her.

Vivienne sank onto the plush bed, the soft fabric enveloping her tired body. The old springs beneath her groaned with each movement, protesting their duty to hold her weight. She squeezed her eyes shut, attempting to calm her pounding heart, as the harsh reality of her new life sunk in. The room was silent except for the gentle hum of the air conditioning and the distant sounds of traffic outside. As she lay there, the coolness of the sheets against her skin brought comfort amidst the chaos inside her mind.

As she sat in the dimly lit cottage, the shadows seemed to dance and taunt her. She could sense their looming presence and her heart raced with fear. With a deep breath, she stood up from the creaky armchair and clutched her at her hands, ready to confront whatever dangers may lurk in the old cottage.

Vivienne's eyes lit up. She needed art supplies. The urge to create, to pour her emotions onto a canvas, consumes her, and for a moment, the weight of her past seemed to lift from her shoulders.

Filled with purpose, Vivienne snatched up her tattered bag, its rusted chains jangling loudly. She hoisted it over her shoulder and strode towards the door, the sound of her footsteps resounding through the hollow cottage. Stepping out into the world, she was met with a rush of crisp, autumn air, a refreshing contrast to the musty atmosphere inside. The scent of damp leaves and earth tickled her nose, invigorating her senses as she embarked on her journey.

Stepping onto the bus, Vivienne's heart thumped wildly in her chest as she made her way toward the nearby town of Guisborough. Her eyes were wide with excitement and apprehension, taking in the quaint streets lined with charming shops and friendly faces. It was a stark contrast to the bleak world she had known for so long. She couldn't help but feel a surge of hope and inspiration as she gazed out at the colourful storefronts and bustling crowds. Her eyes darted from window to window, searching for the one place that held the key to her project.

Finally, after searching for what seemed like hours, she had found it - a quaint art supply shop, its large window adorned with an enticing display of brilliant paints and flawless canvases. Vivienne's heart fluttered as she approached the door, her hand trembling slightly before finally resting on the smooth doorknob. With a deep breath to steady her nerves, she pushed the door open, feeling the gentle breeze of a nearby wind chime announcing her arrival into the store's warm and inviting interior.

As she stepped inside, Vivienne was immediately enveloped by the strong scent of fresh paint and the gentle sound of paper being moved. Her eyes widened in wonder as she took in the sight before her - shelves upon shelves lined with brushes of varying thickness and shape, tubes of paint in every hue imaginable, and sketchbooks eagerly waiting to be used. The room seemed to pulsate with creative energy, and her fingers couldn't help but twitch in anticipation of creating something beautiful. Everywhere she looked, inspiration called out to her, begging to be captured on canvas or paper. It was a paradise for any artist, and Vivienne could feel herself getting lost in the endless possibilities that surrounded her.

She gracefully glided through the shop, her slender fingers lightly skimming over the various art supplies on display. She revelled in the textures of the brushes, from soft and fluffy to stiff and coarse, each one holding its own potential for creating beauty. The smooth, cool surfaces of the paints beckoned to her, promising endless possibilities and a spectrum of colours waiting to be brought to life. As she perused the shelves, her mind became a canvas itself, alive with a kaleidoscope of vibrant hues and intricate designs.

She stocked herself with cans of paint and brushes, her excitement growing at the thought of finally decorating her new cottage. Her creative mind buzzed with ideas for a vibrant and detailed mural that would bring life to the blank walls. She could already smell the rich pigments and textures that would soon cover the once-bare surfaces.

Vivienne's arms were laden with an array of art supplies: brushes of various sizes, tubes of vibrant paints, and blank canvases just waiting to be transformed. Her excitement was palpable as she approached the counter, eager to bring her artistic vision to life. The worn wooden surface creaked under the weight of her materials as she carefully placed them down, a sense of purpose filling her chest. The cashier behind the register greeted her with a warm smile, their eyes sparkling with genuine kindness. As Vivienne handed over her hard-earned money, watching her meagre savings dwindle but feeling a sense of fulfilment wash over her, she couldn't help but feel a cool breeze brush against her face and a weight lift off her shoulders.

Vivienne stepped out of line, her bag now heavy with the weight of her newfound treasures. As she made her way back to the exit, the breeze from a small window whispering through her hair, her eyes locked onto the display of paints adjacent to the door. A makeshift sign above read 'local limited edition' - the paints seemingly from a local supplier.

As Vivienne reached for a tube of vibrant cerulean paint, her fingers grazing the smooth metal, an unfamiliar hand brushed against hers, sending a jolt of electricity through her skin. She looked up, startled, and found herself gazing into the emerald eyes of a tall, imposing man. He offered her a warm smile, one not quite reaching his eyes, the corners of which crinkled with kindness, and Vivienne felt ill at ease, able to sense every movement of his body near her.

"Pardon me," the man said, his deep, rich voice resonating through the quiet shop. "I couldn't help but notice your enthusiasm. Are you an artist?"

Vivienne nodded, averting her eyes, a blush creeping up her cheeks as she took in the man's appearance - the designer stubble that framed his chiselled jawline, the flecks of grey in his brown hair that hinted at a life well-lived. "I'm trying to be," she replied, her voice meek. "I just moved into an old cottage in Skinningrove, and I'm hoping to bring some life to it."

The man's eyes softened, a flicker of understanding passing between them. "Ah, you've got old Reaper's Cottage? A noble pursuit," he said, his gaze never leaving hers. "I'm John, by the way. John Bassinger."

"Vivienne Shawcross," she replies, her heart pounding in her chest as she lowers her head, surveying his offered hand through her eyelashes, a hand that she avoided most carefully.

Instead, she bowed her head coquettishly, acknowledging his kind introduction.

As they stood there, surrounded by the vibrant hues of the paints and the soft rustling of the brushes, Vivienne found herself, against almost every instinct, sharing her deepest desires of transforming the quaint cottage. Her voice trembled as she described peeling wallpaper and creaking floorboards that begged to be fixed and replaced. She even mentioned the whispers in the air that sent shivers down her spine, not realising she was talking the poor man's ear off. But instead of seeing anger or boredom on his face, she raised her head to find a kind expression and his eyes intently watching her every movement.

"It sounds like you have quite the task ahead of you," John said, his voice tinged with sad admiration, as he backed away. "But I do not doubt that you'll succeed."

Vivienne felt a warmth bloom in her chest at his words.

"Thank you," she whispered, though she knew he couldn't hear. The bell chimed again, a soft farewell as she stepped back into the grey.

Her steps faltered outside the shop, pulling her thin coat tighter around her body as a gust of cold wind blew by. The second gust of cold wind that followed made her hair whip around her face and sent goosebumps rising on her skin. The grey sky loomed above, bearing down on her like a heavy blanket. It seemed to be watching her with an unblinking gaze, leaving her exposed and vulnerable. She longed to retreat into the safety of the shadows, where she could hide from its judgmental stare. Her feet itched to flee, but she forced herself to remain.

"Vivienne."

The silence was broken by a deep, sorrowful voice that reverberated through the air. John's tall figure emerged from the shop, and she could feel his presence like a protective shield against the cold. His confident stride revealed his strength as he walked towards her, thoughts etched on his face.

"Your project," he began, hands tucked into the pockets of his worn jacket, "it sounds like a beast of a thing." His gaze held hers, steady and unwavering. "I've got some experience with carpentry. Old houses can be... tricky." A half-smile touched his lips, a brief glimmer of contentment.

'Tricky' was a gentle word for the monster that awaited her. Her heart clenched, hope threading through the frayed edges of her resolve. "You would help?" The words hung, fragile as spider silk between them.

"Would and will." He nodded once, decisive. "Can't let you face such a battle alone."

Alone. The word echoed, a familiar ghost in her mind. Standing before him, relief surged – a sudden, wild tide threatening to undo her. Her breath hitched, gratitude a raw, aching thing within her throat. "Thank you," she managed, slightly louder than she had done before.

Vivienne's eyes widened with surprise and gratitude, her heart swelling at the unexpected offer. She studied John's face, searching for any hint of insincerity, but she found only warmth and sincerity in his green eyes, a reflection of the grief that she knew all too well. But still, her trust faltered.

"I..." Vivienne began, her voice trembling with emotion. "I would be honoured to have your help, John. Thank you... for your kindness."

Vivienne nodded, her eyes glistening with unshed tears. She reached out, firmly shaking his hand this time, a faint impression of a smile sneaking its way onto her face.

With a final, bittersweet squeeze of John's hand, Vivienne reluctantly bid him farewell and began her journey back to the quaint cottage nestled in the heart of the countryside. Her steps were light but purposeful, each stride bringing her closer to the new life that awaited her. The sun painted the sky with hues of pink and orange, casting a warm glow over the countryside. Vivienne's heart beat faster as she imagined all the possibilities ahead, a fire ignited within her as she took in the picturesque landscape around her.

As she inched closer to the dilapidated door, a sudden and intense chill gripped her body, as if a thousand writhing insects were crawling over her skin, leaving trails of pinpricks in their wake. She froze, her hand trembling as it hovered just above the rusted handle, afraid to make contact with whatever lay beyond.

It's just the wind, she told herself, shaking off the unease that threatened to settle in her bones. *Nothing more than the whispers of an old house, the creaks and groans of settling wood.*

Vivienne's skin crawled with a sense of foreboding as she entered the room, her instincts screaming at her to turn and flee. The air inside was suffocatingly thick and stagnant, clogging her throat and making it nearly impossible to draw breath. Suddenly the door slammed shut behind her with a deafening clap, reverberating through the lifeless space like a gunshot. Her heart pounded in her chest as she stood frozen in terror, feeling an ominous presence bearing down on her from all sides. Every muscle in her body screamed at her to run, but she fought against the urge with every ounce of willpower she possessed.

Something's not right, she thought, her eyes darting around the room, searching for the source of the unnatural stillness. *It's as if the cottage itself is holding its breath, waiting for something to happen.*

Suddenly, as if in direct response to her darkest thoughts, the once still and lifeless curtains came alive. A violent gust of wind seemed to surge through the room, causing the faded fabric to ripple and dance in a frenzy. Vivienne's heart rattled as she watched in horror, unable to tear her eyes away from the spectacle before her. A chilling whisper filled the air, swirling around her like a taunting spirit. It was a wordless murmur that carried with it a sense of ominous foreboding, stirring up buried fears within her. As the voice grew louder and more distinct, Vivienne's body trembled uncontrollably. Was this some entity trying to communicate with her? Or was it simply a figment of her imagination, brought on by her own fears and doubts? She stood frozen in place, powerless against the force that gripped her. And as the whispered words reached their climax, Vivienne could no longer deny the terrifying truth - she was not alone in this room.

Vivienne took a deep breath, steeling herself against the rising tide of trepidation that threatened to overwhelm her. She knew that this was only the beginning, that the challenges ahead would test her in ways she had never been tested before.

With a resolute nod, Vivienne ventured further into the cottage, ready to face whatever lay ahead, to unravel the mysteries that lurked within the walls. The way through was dark and treacherous, and for the first time, it looked as if her fear had been well-founded.

Vivienne's hands trembled as she carefully unpacked her art supplies, her sharp eyes scanning the room for any signs of what was lurking within. The air was thick and charged with an unseen energy, sending tingles down her spine and causing her skin to prickle. It felt as though something or someone was watching her every move, their intense gaze causing a knot of fear to form in her stomach. She could sense the weight of their presence, a heavy force that seemed to press down upon her, making it hard to breathe. Every nerve in her body was on edge, ready to react at the slightest provocation.

Focus, she told herself firmly, arms clutching each other to soothe her nerves. *You can't let fear control you. Not now, not ever.*

With shaking fingers, Vivienne reached for her paintbrush, the cool, smooth wood of the handle a comforting weight in her hand. She dipped the brush into a vibrant red, watching as the colour seeped across the bristles like a drop of blood in water.

The brush moved almost of its own accord across the blank wall, guided by some unseen force that seemed to flow from her. Her vision narrowed, her expression blank, her focus honing in like a microscope on a specimen.

As the minutes ticked by, the wall came alive with colour and form, a swirling maelstrom of reds, blues, and golds that seemed to pulse. Vivienne stepped back, her fingers moving awkwardly, and took in the sight of her creation.

It's beautiful, she thought, a faint smile tugging at the corners of her lips. *And it's mine. No matter what happens, no one can take this away from me.*

A shiver ran down her spine as she felt a cold hand press against the small of her back. Her posture immediately straightened in response, her muscles coiled like a spring ready to release. Desperately trying to maintain focus, she fixated on a point on the wall, refusing to let her eyes stray to the edges of her peripheral vision where danger may lurk.

It's here again, she thought, her heart hammering in her chest.

She turned sharply, looking around the room, her eyes wide and fearful, but there was nothing to be seen. Only the faint creaking of the floorboards and the whisper of the wind through the cracks in the walls broke the eerie silence.

She turned back to the wall, feeling her pulse in her fingers and ears. Swallowing hard, she reapplied her brush, continuing to translate her mind onto the space.

As she painted, the mural on the wall began to take shape, a riot of colour and light that seemed to break through the atmosphere, like magic depicted in 70s films. Vivienne lost herself in the work, her mind focused solely on the task at hand, as if by sheer force of will she could keep the darkness at bay.

Finally, after what seemed an eternity, she stepped back from the wall, her eyes tracing the lines and curves of the mural that now adorned the hallway. It was far more than she had imagined, a masterpiece if she could be so bold, and Vivienne felt a sense of pride and accomplishment wash over her.

As she leaned in, her eyes bulged with a frenzied intensity, hungrily devouring every inch of the swirling colours and abstract shapes. But amidst the chaotic beauty, she spotted something else hidden within - a half-face, dark and sinister, lurking just beneath the surface. With a fierce determination, she reached out and pressed her thumb against the image, smearing it with a thick, tar-like substance that oozed from her touch like poison. She then dragged her tainted thumb across the canvas, leaving behind a trail of black smudges that blended into her painting like a twisted signature. The figure now seemed to come alive, emanating an eerie aura that sent spine-tingling chills coursing through her body.

She had not even bought black paint.

Vivienne's heart paused, her face white with fear, but she refused to let it consume her.

No matter what happens, she thought, her jaw set, *I will not let this place break me. I will make it my own, and I will find a way to banish the darkness that haunts it.*

With that thought, Vivienne turned away from the mural, her mind already racing with plans for other such works in the house, resolving to write a plan when her mind was fresh and not addled by the tricks of the cottage.

Exhausted, Vivienne collapsed onto the worn-out couch, the springs panging beneath her weight. Her eyelids grew heavy, the brush slipping from her paint-stained fingers as they unfurled like petals in the sun. The mural seems to shimmer in the fading light, the colours dancing and swirling together around the creepy image.

Is this what it feels like to create something beautiful? Vivienne wondered, her thoughts drifting like gossamer on the wind. *To pour your heart and soul into a work, to make something that will endure long after you are gone?*

As her heavy eyelids slowly descended, Vivienne's mind began to wander once again. A flurry of fragmented images danced behind her closed lids, each one a vivid and haunting picture from her past. She saw herself as a small, scared child, curled up in a corner of a desolate, chilly room, the shadows looming over her like menacing giants. She could almost feel the cold seeping into her bones. And then, in a flash, she was confronted with the faces of the men who had caused her so much pain and anguish. Their twisted and sinister expressions were burned into her memory, their dark eyes gleaming with malice and cruelty. But amidst all this darkness, there was something else lurking, something that made her heart race and her blood run akin to ice.

A towering and menacing figure loomed over her like a living shadow, its eyes blazing with an otherworldly fire that seemed to penetrate her very soul. Its scales, as dark as obsidian and sharp as razors, caught the faint light in the darkness and gleamed with a deadly edge. Vivienne's throat constricted with terror, but she could only let out a strangled gasp as the creature reached out with a clawed hand toward her frozen form. She willed her legs to move, to run, to escape, but they remained rooted to the spot as if under some powerful spell from this monstrous being.

This is just a dream, she told herself, even as the figure reached out again, its touch searing her skin like fire, leaving tar in its wake. *It's not real, it can't hurt me.*

But deep down, she knew it was a warning, a glimpse of the challenges ahead. And as she succumbed to the exhaustion that threatened to overwhelm her, she could not help but wonder what horrors the future held in store.

CHAPTER 4

I'm Watching You and so is She

Narrator's Note 11.47.3.3 - Loneliness is often the toll charge paid for the tangled road we take.

The soft glow of dawn illuminated the room through a lace-curtained window, casting warm shadows across Vivienne's paint-splattered smock. She eagerly arranged her brushes on the table, carefully inspecting each for stray bristles or dried paint. Outside, birds chirped and cars hummed by, but Vivienne was lost in her own world as she took in the intoxicating smell of acrylics and turpentine. Her fingers itched to start creating as she gazed out at the vibrant colours of the blooming garden just beyond the open window.

The paints came next, carried by the bright sunlight that made their colours sparkle and come to life. Vivienne's eyes widened with excitement as she took in the sight of the small pots filled with vibrant crimson, deep cobalt, and rich emerald hues. She couldn't resist dipping her pinky finger into the cool, velvety green paint, feeling its thick texture suffocate her skin.

With slow and deliberate movements, she stepped back from the wall, her eyes scanning its surface. The once pristine paint was now marred by an intricate web of cracks and stains, giving it a worn and aged appearance. Her gaze fell upon the unexplainable image from yesterday, its figure no longer smudged but as clear and vibrant as ever. Vivienne reached for an old dishcloth to clean her finger before bringing her face close to the character, stopping at eye level with the curious creature on the wall. Its eyes seemed to blink at her, almost alive in their eternal stare. Suddenly overwhelmed, Vivienne moved her head back sharply, closing her eyes in bewilderment as her breathing became shallow. In a fit of frustration, she grabbed the biggest brush on the table and clumsily coated it in white paint. With swift and angry strokes, she pasted over the face until not even a sliver of black remained visible beneath the thick layer of paint. Her chest heaved as she stood back to examine her work, still unable to comprehend the mysterious image before her.

"What are you painting, my dear?"

The voice, a gentle whisper that seemed to float in the air, startled Vivienne from her outburst. She spun around, her eyes scanning the empty room for the source of the mysterious sound. The lingering scent of patchouli filled her nostrils, adding to the otherworldly atmosphere. It was as if a spirit had passed through, leaving only traces of its presence.

"I... I don't know yet," Vivienne admitted quietly. "Something to make sense of all this, I suppose. Something to leave behind."

Tears escaped their pools and slipped down Vivienne's cheek, leaving a glistening trail in its wake. She nodded, unable to speak past the painful lump in her throat, and turned back to the wall.

With a deep, steadying breath, she raised her sleeves to wipe away the tears that had streamed down her cheeks. Her fingers trembled as she reached for an already well-worn brush, its bristles stained with remnants of past creations. She carefully dipped it into the vibrant paint, mesmerised by how the colour seemed to cling to the brush like a barnacle to a ship.

Vivienne stood before the blank wall, taking in every inch of it before reaching out with a steady hand. As her fingers grazed the surface, she felt a pang in her chest, a familiar sensation that made her pause and rub at the spot above her heart. It wasn't the same tension as before, but it was enough to make her hesitate before making the first mark.

The brush met the wall, and Vivienne's hand moved in natural flowing strokes. The crimson paint glided across the surface, leaving a bold, sweeping stroke in its wake. She dug the brush into the crevices of the wall, the wall seemingly damaged where the image once was, the bristles becoming hot to the touch.

As she painted, Vivienne's mind was taken hostage by her haunting past. The memories swirled relentlessly, clawing at her psyche with an insatiable hunger for control - the searing agony, the paralysing terror, the suffocating sense of hopelessness that had driven her to the brink of self-destruction. She fought to keep them at bay, but they crept closer and closer, threatening to engulf her in a tidal wave of despair.

She remembered the feeling of rough, calloused hands on her skin, the sound of cruel laughter echoing in her ears. She shrank where she stood, pulling her extremities close to her, the sense of manipulation that had settled over her like a shroud. Feeling the creature's eyes staring at her from below the imagery she had now covered it with, she remembered the moment when she had finally broken and the weight of it all had become too much to bear. Then she had sought solace in the oblivion of death.

An overwhelming sense of unexplainable power weighed down on her, suffocating her like a puppet controlled by invisible, malign strings. She could feel the weight of someone else's will pressing against her own, manipulating her every move. With a blank expression, she stood before the wall, meticulously painting each detail with a small brush, her body moving on autopilot as if disconnected from her mind. The room felt thick with mystery and danger, and she couldn't shake the feeling that something sinister lurked beyond her grasp.

The crimson paint flowed like blood. It was a reminder that, despite everything, she was still alive, still breathing, and capable of creating something in the face of unimaginable darkness.

As she deftly added layers of deep, rich blue to the canvas, intertwining them with bold strokes of fiery red, a sudden howling wind burst through a cracked window. The shards shattered upon impact, creating a tinkling chorus that echoed through the room. As the wind mixed with the wet paint still clinging to the wall, it swirled and danced in an otherworldly ballet. The once familiar room transformed into a chaotic scene, the colours, and elements colliding and melding together in an odd yet mesmerising motif. The wall was a dizzying swirl of red and blue, mimicking the emotions tearing through the house. It was as if the walls themselves were trying to contain the chaos within.

Her mind wandered to the warm and welcoming voice she had heard earlier, starkly different from the chaos and darkness that consumed the rest of the house. It was almost as if the voice was in direct opposition to everything else, alluring and tempting her with its mysterious nature. She couldn't help but wonder what it wanted from her, and why it seemed to have an unsettling understanding of her innermost thoughts. Its presence both comforted and unnerved her, like a flickering flame in a sea of shadows.

With trembling hands, Vivienne stepped back to survey her masterpiece. The mural sprawled across the wall before her like a living, breathing entity. Each stroke of paint was a piece of her soul, a reflection of her deepest desires and fears. A wailing woman in vibrant primary colours stood on the edge, her tormented expression bleeding into the tempest depicted over the house. The swirling clouds now resembled a dark mausoleum, foreboding and ominous. Vivienne's heart raced with a mix of exhilaration and fear. It was a risk, she knew, to expose herself so fully, to lay bare the scars that marred her psyche.

But in that moment, as she gazed upon the portrayal, symbiotic to the house and its foibles, and the chaotic beauty of her creation, Vivienne felt a warmth grow in her abdomen and her eyes betrayed a weary smile.

The colours blended and seeped into one another, creating an otherworldly effect as if the wall itself was alive. The crimson and deep blue swirled together in a mesmerising dance, while the splashes of vibrant yellow seemed to pulse with a life of their own. It was as if the mural was a living, breathing entity, a manifestation. A manifestation that evidently wished for its own face, as there it was, beneath the colours in the storm, the face that she had done her best to cover. This time it wasn't as sharp a picture, the black not seen, just the colours reforming its beast-like eyes.

The house would watch.

As the mural neared completion, Vivienne's heart distended with a bittersweet mixture of pride and sorrow. She knows that this creation, this outpouring of her soul, will be her legacy. A legacy someone was signalling they wanted to be a part of, and she did not have the strength to refuse it a third time.

With a determined grunting, she dragged the old, ever-rocking chair across the creaky wooden floor from its corner to her desired spot. The floorboards groaned and protested under the weight and movement. She carefully prepared a cup of steaming tea, adding just the right amount of honey and cream for her taste. Finally, with a satisfied sigh, she settled into the chair opposite the painting that would be her pride and joy. A content smile spread across her face as she took in every brushstroke and colour.

"It's magnificent," a deep, familiar voice came from behind her.

She turned to see John leaning against the wooden frame of the doorway, his piercing green eyes transfixed on the mural in front of them. The corners of his mouth were slightly downturned, giving away a mixture of awe and deep sorrow that mirrored her own emotions.

"Thank you," Vivienne smiled. "I wanted to create something beautiful, something that would last..."

Her words trailed off as a wave of emotion threatened to overwhelm her. John stepped forward, placing a comforting hand on her shoulder, quickly removing it as he felt her tense beneath his fingers.

"You've done that and more," he said softly. "This mural... it's a part of you, Vivienne..."

He could not bring himself to finish the sentence, but Vivienne understood.

She knew that her time was running out, that the disease that ravaged her body would soon claim her life. There would be no comfort, no generosity, for it was her mind that was diseased and in succumbing they would not call her brave. They would call her weak. No matter how much she logically recognised the misbelief at the heart of these most tragic thoughts, she could not change them. But at that moment, standing before the mural that she had poured her heart and soul into, with John examining it intently, the thoughts ebbed away and she felt content, like a reader on a sun lounger, basking in the heat.

"I don't want to be forgotten," she whispered, her voice trembling with emotion. "I want people to know that I was here, that I mattered…"

John stood directly behind her, his presence akin to a hug, though no contact was made. He considered stroking the back of her hair but had already sensed her nervousness around being touched. He did not know how else to comfort her, the strangeness of her company becoming painfully apparent.

"You'll not be forgotten, I foresee great things well beyond these four walls for you. You're young, you have time." John sighed deeply.

With a crackle of leaves, they both heard something in the outermost room. Something pacing. Vivienne's head shook in disbelief as she stood up from her seat, pushing it to the side with a screech across the wooden floor.

"Bloody house," she cursed, "thank you for coming to help, I don't know whether it is worth you having a look around and seeing what you think. To be honest, I don't know where to start on the practical stuff... just as well we bumped into each other really...".

"Well I am here to help, so let me see what we are working with." John nodded, meandering off to explore the house. Vivienne smiled briefly as she watched him leave the room, his eyes surveying, his hands clasped behind his back. She picked up the small brush she had propped up on the side of a paint tube, and resolved to add further details before she lost the light.

As the fiery sun descended, casting a deep orange glow through the small cottage windows, Vivienne's brush strokes slowed to a halt. Her eyes burned from hours of intense concentration and her limbs felt heavy. She couldn't fight the exhaustion any longer and her form shrank as she curled up on the spot, mimicking a fetal position in a reflexive response to the day's work. The room was now enveloped in an eerie half-light, shadows dancing on the walls.

John reappeared in the doorway, his eyes fixed on Vivienne's hunched form and the way her delicate hands shook with each stroke of the brush. He could see the toll this labour of love was taking on her fragile body, and yet, he could not bring himself to intervene, to tear her away from the one thing that seemed to bestow her a modicum of peace.

"You need to rest, Vivienne," he said softly, his voice laced with concern. "You've been at this for hours."

Vivienne shook her head, her eyes never leaving the mural. "Need to finish it today, before the feeling wanes"

John's heart clenched at her words, the finality of them hitting him like a physical blow. He could see that something was eating away at her, something existential. Though he had not given it much thought, the haunting look on her face and the gravity of the few words she spoke, was part of the reason he had felt compelled to offer help. A familiar stubbornness of spirit that struck a chord.

He stepped closer, approaching with the palms of his hands open and unencumbered, allowing her to track every movement she made. "I understand," he concedes, his voice thick with emotion. "But please, Vivienne, don't push yourself too hard. You need your strength."

Vivienne moved closer, leaning into his touch awkwardly, movements stiff. "I know," she replies breathily, her chest visibly rising and falling considerably. "But I fear that if I stop now, I may never find the courage to start again."

Vivienne's gaze remained fixed upon the mural, her eyes tracing the intricate patterns and swirling colours that now adorned the once-barren wall.

"It's a masterpiece," John murmurs, his mouth a hair's breadth away from her ear. "You've captured something rather otherworldly..."

He trails off, sensing the description threw up more questions than she had answered. Vivienne's hands, no longer shaking, set her brush down, her fingers stained. She turned to face him, her eyes watery.

"Okay," she said softly, her voice unsure.

"Okay," she repeated, louder with certainty.

John reached out, but she had already fled his touch, back into the safety of her chair.

"Well, in looking at the cottage, there are several things I could help with, the woodwork is in awful condition particularly. I could maybe start with that? Looking at your artwork, I think a very dark wood would work best..." John gestured to the mural.

"As dark as my soul? How apt," she chuckled, the droll humour causing John to raise an eyebrow. "Sounds good"

John smirked, the surprise still not abated, and backed out of the room.

"I'll organise some stuff then, and I'll come back and crack on" he called out. "See you then?"

"See you then" she repeated back to him, an affability existing in her voice that had not been there before.

As Vivienne heard the door close, all the warmth she had felt dissipated, silence smothering the mirth that had been there just seconds ago. The room greyed and cooled before her and the wind, once welcome, now cold and sharp like steel. She looked at the mural, her eyes drawn to the face that had been there before, its features becoming clearer and clearer.

With an alarming hiss from something close beside her, the candle abruptly lost its flame and Vivienne closed her eyes. The only thing worse than a terrifying unseen thing was a terrifying seen thing.

CHAPTER 5

You Won't Have Her Bones Either

Narrator's Note 8.5.2.11 - Each individual is most definitely a pentimento, but of how many layers will probably never be truly known.

John's house exuded a picturesque charm, with its quaint little gate and hanging baskets overflowing with vibrant flowers. A sign adorned the front of the house, displaying the name 'Garden Cottage' in cheerful lettering. The pastel-toned mailbox stood proudly next to the gate, a reminder of simpler times.

But upon closer inspection, it was clear that this idyllic facade was but an illusion. The once-lively blooms in the hanging baskets had wilted and drooped, their malnourished stems unable to support their weight. The wooden gate showed signs of decay, half of it covered in a thick layer of green moss while the other half was held together by fraying fishing rope. The house sign had faded beyond recognition and the paint on the mailbox had cracked and peeled, its opening obstructed by a waterlogged piece of cardboard.

'In Loving Memory, Odelia' it read, the text alongside a photo of a woman, stunning in a wedding dress.

Inside the house, the space was enveloped in a chaotic mess. Towers of dusty books teetered precariously, threatening to topple over at any moment. Piles of letters and clothes were scattered haphazardly, creating a maze-like path through the cluttered living space. Old bottles and plates lay forgotten on the floor, adding to the overwhelming sense of disarray. With a sigh, John kicked off his shoes in the doorway and flung his jacket onto a pile of books, desperate for some semblance of order. The adrenaline rush from the afternoon had faded, leaving him drained and exhausted. As he trudged through the maze of belongings into the lounge, he nearly stumbled over an abandoned bowl on the floor. But it wasn't just the mess that stopped him in his tracks; it was something else entirely - something surprising and unexpected.

There stood a ghostly form, an unearthly being, giving off chill where the living would give off heat. It felt anomalous, unfamiliar, yet John knew instantly what, or rather who, stood before him. There was no mistaking his wife for anyone else, even if in death.

"Sweetheart?" he managed to ask, his heart threatening to leap out of his open mouth.

Odelia turned to look at him, the apparition of her extraordinarily long hair rippling, as if in water. She did not offer a reply but started to sob, her tears rolling off her face and dissolving to nothing. He moved towards her hesitantly, absolutely perplexed and enamoured, and with the movement she too dissolved to nothing as her tears had done.

John sank back onto the worn leather sofa, the fabric cold against his skin. He stared at the empty space where Odelia had stood, his eyes tracing the invisible contours of her ghostly form. The room seemed to contract around him, the walls pressing in, suffocating in their proximity.

He drew a shuddering breath, the air thick and stale in his lungs. The silence was a tangible presence, broken only by the erratic rhythm of his heartbeat. It echoed in his ears, a mocking reminder of his persistent existence.

"Why?" he asked the vacant room, his voice rough with disuse. "Why did you leave me?"

The questions hung unanswered, swallowed by nothingness. He closed his eyes, his head falling back against the cushions. The memories assailed him, relentless in their clarity. Odelia's laughter, her gentle touch, the way her eyes sparkled with mischief and love. Each image was a knife's twist in his gut, a fresh wave of pain crashing over him.

"I can't do this without you," he confessed, his words a broken whisper. "I don't know how to be alone."

The admission tasted bitter on his tongue, a weakness he couldn't afford. He was the unflappable detective, the man who had stared down the barrel of a gun without flinching. But here, in the solitude of his grief, he was stripped bare, reduced to a shell of his former self.

He forced his eyes open, his gaze drifting to the framed photograph on the mantelpiece. Odelia smiled back at him, her face radiant with joy. It had been taken on their honeymoon, a moment frozen in time, a promise of forever that had been shattered too soon.

"I miss you," he said, the words catching in his throat. "I miss you so damn much."

The house creaked in response, a mournful sigh that echoed his own. He listened to his ragged breathing, each inhalation a struggle against the weight of his sorrow. The minutes ticked by, marked only by the distant chime of the grandfather clock in the hallway.

A sudden chill swept through the room, raising goosebumps on John's skin. The air seemed to shimmer and distort, as if something otherworldly was about to appear. And indeed it did - a pale, ethereal form materialised before him, its presence sending a shiver down his spine. Odelia's ghost hovered mere feet away, her translucent figure swaying gently as if caught in an unseen breeze. Her dress, once flowy and vibrant, now appeared tattered and faded with time. But what caught John's attention was the thin veil draped over her head, fluttering like a moth's wings in the soft light. As it lifted slightly, he caught a glimpse of the familiar headband beneath, reminiscent of the iconic Girl with the Pearl Earring painting. It was both haunting and beautiful at the same time.

John's breath caught in his throat, his eyes widening in disbelief. "Odelia?" he whispered, his voice trembling.

The ghost tilted her head, a sarcastic smile playing on her translucent lips. "Well, well, well," she drawled, her aristocratic tone echoing in the room. "If it isn't my dear husband, wallowing in his misery."

John flinched at her words, a fresh wave of guilt washing over him. "I... I don't know what to do without you," he admitted, his voice raw with emotion.

Odelia drifted closer, her pale hand reaching to caress John's cheek. He shivered at the icy touch, a stark reminder of the chasm between life and death. "Oh, darling," she purred, her tone teasing, "you always were a bit of a drama queen."

Despite the heaviness in his heart, John couldn't help but chuckle. It was so like Odelia to mock him, even in the face of his grief. "I thought I was the strong, silent type," he retorted, a faint smile tugging at his lips.

"Silent, yes," Odelia agreed, her ghostly eyes sparkling with mirth. "But strong? That remains to be seen."

John's smile faded, his sorrow crashing down upon him once more. "I'm trying, Odelia," he said, his voice barely above a whisper. "But it's so hard without you."

The ghost's expression softened, a flicker of sympathy crossing her ethereal features. "I know, my love," she murmured, her voice a soothing balm to his battered soul. "But you must find a way. For both of us."

John blinked back unshed tears as he met Odelia's ethereal gaze. "Why did you do it?" he asked, his voice trembling. "Why did you leave me?" The unspoken accusation hung heavy in the air between them.

Odelia seemed to shimmer, her edges blurring as if she might disappear at any moment. "I couldn't bear the pain any longer," she confessed, her words weighted with sorrow and regret. "The darkness within me grew until it consumed everything."

A single tear escaped John's eye, trailing down his weathered cheek. He clenched his fists, his knuckles turning white with the effort. "I should have been there for you," he said, his voice breaking. "I should have seen the signs, done something..."

Odelia shook her head, her veil fluttering with the movement. "It's not your fault, John," she assured him, her tone gentle yet firm. "I made my choice, and I alone bear the consequences."

John's shoulders slumped, the weight of his grief threatening to crush him. He had spent countless sleepless nights replaying every moment, every conversation, searching for the clues he had missed. The signs that his beloved wife was slipping away from him, lost in a sea he couldn't even begin to comprehend.

Odelia's ghostly hand reached out, hovering just above John's heart. "You have a way to move forward, I've been watching" she urged, her voice a soothing whisper. "You are stronger than you know, John Bassinger. You have so much life left to live."

John's heart ached, torn between the desire to cling to his grief and the knowledge that Odelia was right. He had to find a way to move forward, to honour her memory by living the life she no longer could.

"I'll try," he promised, his voice hoarse.

She smiled, a bittersweet expression that spoke of love and loss in equal measure. "That's all I ask, my darling," she murmured, her form fading.

As Odelia disappeared, John was left alone once more, the room resuming closing in around him. He drew in a shuddering breath, his body constricted by his emotions and the promise he had made.

John's stiff joints creaked as he rose from his chair. He shuffled towards the window, his gaze fixated on the moonlit garden just beyond the glass. The familiar scent of Odelia's prized roses filled his nostrils and he couldn't help but smile at the memory of her tending to them with such devotion. Their delicate petals danced in the cool night air, a reminder of her gentle touch that he would never truly feel again.

He couldn't help but brush his hand along the smooth wooden banister, a project they had completed together during their first year in the house. He paused in the living room, where they had spent countless nights cuddled up on the couch watching their favourite shows. The kitchen held memories of laughter and burnt dinners as they navigated learning how to cook together. Each room was a bittersweet reminder of the life and home they had built together, now filled with emptiness and echoes of Odelia's absence.

And yet, as he gazed out at the garden, it wasn't sadness he felt so acutely. This was their home, the one place where he had always felt safe and loved. He couldn't let his grief take that away from him too.

As he moved through the room, John's fingers trailed along the spines of the books they had collected over the years, the worn leather and faded pages a testament to the life they had lived. He would start there, he decided, with the stories they had loved, the ones that had brought them comfort and joy in their darkest moments.

For the first time since Odelia's death, John sat and opened a book. He began reading, distress giving way to confusion. He read the first page aloud, with nobody to hear it but the walls, the cogs in his brain turning. He closed the book with a thud, examining the cover.

'Peter and Wendy' it read in gold foiling.

"Peter Pan!" he exclaimed with incredulity, starting to chuckle.

"Of course it's Peter Pan, trying to tell me something, are we Sweetheart?" he said, waving the book around before putting it down. The acknowledgement of her already started to poison the moment, and he picked up the bottle of whiskey sitting next to the sofa on the floor, hugging it close. Odelia reappeared, concern screaming from her features.

John's voice trembled as he spoke, his words heavy with regret and self-blame. "I should have seen the signs, Odelia. It is no use to tell me otherwise. I should have been there for you when you needed me most." His eyes, green, now dulled by sorrow, gazed at the ethereal form of his late wife.

Odelia reached out, her translucent hand hovering just above John's cheek. "You couldn't have known, my love. I hid my pain well, even from you." Her voice, though soft and echoing, was tinged with sadness.

"But I was a detective, for God's sake!" John's fist clenched, his knuckles turning white. "I should have noticed something, anything. I failed you, Odelia. I failed to save you." His shoulders shook as he fought back the tears that threatened to spill.

Exhaustion, both physical and emotional, threatened to end John. His once strong frame seemed to shrink under the burden of his grief. "I'm so tired, Odelia. Tired of the guilt, the pain, the emptiness." His words came in short, choppy sentences, as if each one required a tremendous effort.

Odelia circled John, her body peeking out of the dress. "You must forgive yourself, John. You cannot carry this guilt forever." Her voice was gentle, yet firm. "I made my choice, and it was not your fault."

John shook his head, his eyes squeezing shut as he tried to block out the memories that haunted him. The moments he had missed, the signs he had overlooked, the chances he had lost to save his beloved wife. "I can't, Odelia. I can't forgive myself. Not yet, not ever."

The weight of his loss pressed down upon him, suffocating in its intensity. The once comforting walls of his home now seemed to close in around him, a stark reminder of the emptiness that pervaded every corner. The very safety and familiarity that John had always found solace in now served as a bitter contrast to the aching void left by Odelia's absence.

"Oh, my darling," Odelia whispered, her ethereal form drawing closer to him. "This house, our home, holds so many memories. Memories of our love, our laughter, our dreams." She moved as if incapable of stillness. "But it is not a prison. You must not let it become one."

John's eyes flickered open, meeting Odelia's ghostly gaze. The sorrow in her eyes mirrored his own, a shared pain that transcended the boundaries of life and death. "I don't know how to go on without you, Odelia. This house, it's all I have left of you, of us."

Odelia's lips curved into a sad smile. "No, my love. You have so much more. The cycle of life stops for no one." Her voice grew stronger, more insistent.

John's body slowly rose from the ground, as if pulled up by an unseen energy. Odelia approached him, her form glowing with a soft light that enveloped him in a warm embrace. Though he felt no physical touch, John could sense the love and comfort emanating from her being. It was as if her very presence was lifting him up.

And yet, as the moment drew to a close, John knew that this reprieve was fleeting. The grief that had consumed him for so long would not be vanquished so easily, no matter how much he distracted himself. And Vivienne was a most healthy distraction.

CHAPTER 6

Dark Age or Rotting Away?

Narrator's Journey Note 11.36.4.12 - Everything has a dark side.

John's calloused and weathered hand clenched tightly around the rusted iron handle, his toolbox weighing heavily in the other. With a creak and a groan, the door opened, revealing the worn and age-old entryway of Vivienne's cottage. The hinges strained under the door, protesting with every movement.

A thick silence draped over John like a musty cloak as he stepped inside. Dust motes danced in the dim light filtering through the patched-up window panes. His footsteps echoed hollowly on the decaying floorboards, each step echoing like a heavy heartbeat in the otherwise silent room. The chill in the air clung to his skin, causing his breath to mist before him.

Suddenly, without warning, the door slammed shut behind him with a deafening bang. John spun around, his heart pounding in his chest. The lock clicked into place with an eerie finality, trapping him inside. He was alone, at the mercy of whatever unseen force had closed the door.

"Vivienne?" he called out, to no avail.

As John stepped forward, a floorboard groaned under his weight, betraying his presence. He froze, senses suddenly heightened in the eerie silence. The shadows seemed alive, twisting and contorting across the peeling wallpaper in grotesque shapes. The dim light fixtures overhead flickered and sputtered, casting an otherworldly glow that pulsed with each flicker, possessed by some unseen force. Goosebumps prickled across John's skin as he stood there, feeling the weight of the creepy atmosphere pressing down on him.

John's grip tightened on his toolbox, knuckles white. The rational part of his mind, honed by years as a detective, grappled with the unease slithering down his spine. There had to be a logical explanation. Old wiring, drafts from broken windows. Yet the primal instinct deep within, an ancestral memory from when mankind huddled around fires while monsters prowled the dark, whispered otherwise.

"It's just an old house," John muttered, his deep baritone seeming to swallow the words rather than project them. Speaking aloud felt blasphemous somehow, like shouting in a crypt.

With a deep breath, he willed his feet to move forward. Slowly, he took one step, then another. As his boots made contact with the ground, dust clouds rose around him, catching the light and creating an otherworldly sparkle. Despite the biting cold air, John could feel beads of sweat forming on his forehead.

The once bustling kitchen was now a desolate ruin of shattered crockery and mildewed countertops. The stench of mould and decay hung thick in the air, making breathing a slog. The dining room chairs stood empty, their velvet upholstery faded and riddled with holes from moths. In the parlour, a black void loomed where the hearth used to be, the charred bricks resembling rotted teeth in a gaping mouth.

Everywhere John looked, there was only that same haunting, watchful silence. It seemed to permeate every inch of the cottage, suffocating in its all-encompassing stillness. Even his own breaths sounded too loud in his ears against the eerie hush of the house.

A sudden gust of wind cut through, a sharp whistle that sounded like a rasping exhale. John's senses were on high alert as the hair on the back of his neck stood on end. He spun around, half-expecting to come face to face with a ghostly figure reaching out with desperate hands.

But there was nothing. Only the gloom and dust that clung to every surface, suffocating and heavy. As he took in his surroundings, John felt a wave of dread wash over him, pressing down on his chest.

His reflection in the cracked mirror showed a face that was drawn and haggard, barely recognizable as his own. The shadows seemed to play tricks on his features, distorting them into something dark and unfamiliar.

Grief did that to a man. Carved him out from the inside until only a husk remained. Since Odelia's death, John had wandered through his days like a sleepwalker, numb and disconnected. Food turned to ashes in his mouth. Laughter sounded distant and distorted, as if from underwater. Only the guilt remained, sharp and bright as a shard of glass.

Now, standing alone in the decaying ruin of Vivienne's house, John felt the weight of all he had lost pressing down upon him. The toolbox dragged at his arm, suddenly leaden. What was the point of fixing this place? What could he possibly hope to accomplish, shattered as he was?

But no. He had made a promise. To Vivienne, and himself. He would see this through, no matter how his mind shrank from the task.

Squaring his shoulders, John stepped forward into the waiting shadows.

With a grunt, John hefted his heavy toolbox onto the ancient, rickety table. The old wood groaned and creaked in protest as if it had been waiting for this moment to collapse. The sound reverberated through the empty rooms, bouncing off the bare walls and adding to the eerie quiet. John winced, bracing himself for an imminent collapse, but to his surprise, the aged table held on by a thread. The strain of supporting his toolbox was evident in its strained joints and splintered surface. It was a miracle it had survived this long.

With precise, almost mechanical movements, he unpacked his tools from their worn leather case. One by one, he laid them out in perfectly straight rows on the workbench before him. This familiar ritual was a source of comfort to him, a way to push back the ever-present darkness that threatened to engulf his mind. Each tool had its designated spot, and its specific purpose - the hammer, the wrench, the screwdriver, and the pliers. These tools were organised and predictable. Unlike him.

"Focus, John," he muttered, his voice a raw scrape in the silence. "One thing at a time."

He reached for the hammer, his calloused fingers curling around the worn wooden handle. The metal head gleamed dully in the flickering light of the workshop. How often had he held a hammer like this one, working alongside Odelia on one of her endless projects? The memories slammed into him with vicious force, each sharp and vivid.

Odelia, her infectious laughter ringing out as she wielded a paintbrush dripping with sunny yellow paint. Odelia, her face streaked with sawdust and sweat as she triumphantly drove the final nail into their new bookshelf. Odelia, her eyes bright with love and mischief as she playfully snatched the hammer from his hand and pulled him in for a kiss.

John squeezed his eyes shut against the onslaught of emotions, his grip tightening convulsively on the hammer. The pain in his chest was an all-consuming ache, tearing at his heart and stealing his breath. But amidst the agony, he welcomed it.

"I miss you," he whispered, a broken plea in the darkness. "I miss you so damn much."

But there was no answer. There never would be again.

Abruptly, the lights above him began to flicker and stutter, casting distorted shadows that seemed to reach out for John with gnarled, spectral fingers. The air in the room grew dense and suffocating, wrapping around him like a weighty presence.

He gasped for air, the musty scent of age and dust filling his lungs. A metallic tang lingered in the air, hinting at something more sinister. Goosebumps rose on his skin, a primal response to the bone-chilling cold that seemed to seep through every inch of his body.

"Get it together, Bassinger," he growled, his deep voice echoing hollowly in the empty room. "You've got a job to do."

Forcing himself to move, he began to assess the extent of the renovation needed. The peeling wallpaper, like flayed skin, hung in tatters from the walls. The floorboards sagged under his weight, groaning with each step he took. Water stains marred the once-white ceiling, resembling ominous clouds above a stormy sea. It was worse than he had anticipated, a desolate shell of its former self that mirrored the shattered remnants of his own life.

As he worked, the unsettling presence in the house seemed to grow bolder, more malevolent. The lights flickered with increasing violence, strobing erratically and casting twisted shadows that danced and writhed like tortured souls. The air grew colder, heavy with a sense of dread that seeped into his bones, his blood, his very marrow.

Suddenly, the door creaked open with a sound like the groan of a dying man. John whirled around, his heart pounding a frantic rhythm against his ribs. Beyond the gaping doorway, the bleak landscape splayed out before him - dead trees reaching towards an ominously dark sky, fields shrouded in thick mist. The air was heavy with foreboding and the promise of an impending storm, adding to the eerie atmosphere of this abandoned place.

"Vivienne?" he called again, thinking she was back from her errands.

A violent gust of icy wind tore through the small cottage, slamming into him with a force that felt like a physical blow. It ripped the warmth from his body and stole the air he breathed, shivering uncontrollably as his exhalations turned into mist in the frigid air. The chill seeped deep into his bones, numbing him to the core.

"What do you want from me?" he shouted, his voice raw and ragged, swallowed up by the silence. "Why are you doing this?"

But there was no answer, only the mournful wail of the wind and the relentless flickering of the lights. The presence in the house seemed to mock him, to revel in his pain and despair. It was a diabolical force, a twisted entity that fed on suffering and sorrow.

John clenched his jaw, his fists tightening at his sides. He would not be broken. He would not let this thing, this fiendish presence, win. He had made a promise to Vivienne, and he intended to keep it, no matter the cost.

With a calming breath, he returned to his work, the hammer a comforting weight in his hand. The renovation would be long and arduous, but it was a welcome distraction from the gaping void of grief that threatened to consume him. As he surveyed the dilapidated cottage, memories flooded back – laughter echoing through the halls, children playing in the yard, Odelia's gentle touch.

And so, as the lights flickered and the shadows danced, as the icy wind howled through the cottage and the vindictive presence within grew ever more enraged, John worked tirelessly. He poured his anguish into every swing of the hammer, every twist of the wrench, every turn of the screwdriver. This was his battle against darkness.

He would not let the darkness win.

Not this time. Not ever again.

John's hammer struck the decaying boards with a resounding thud, each impact sending a shockwave through his weary arms. The uneven rhythm of his blows echoed through the once quaint cottage, now a decrepit shell of its former self. The walls rumbled in protest, protesting against the cruel and relentless force inflicted upon them.

Dust and splinters danced in the flickering light, a macabre ballet of decay and neglect. Each particle seemed to taunt John, mocking him for his futile efforts to save the dilapidated structure. The air was thick, enveloping him in a woolly cloak of despair.

As he continued to work, the presence in the house seemed to sense his weakness, his vulnerability. It grew bolder and more aggressive, the lights flickering on and off with increasing rapidity. Shadows darted across the room, distorted and grotesque. The air grew even heavier, pressing down upon him like a physical weight, making it hard to breathe, and hard to think.

The faces in the painting above the fireplace seemed to contort and distort as they were observed, moving as if animated by some unseen force. The eyes followed John's every move, their expressions shifting from serene to sinister in an unnerving display.

He refused to give up. With every ounce of strength left in his trembling body, he ripped at the decaying boards with a ferocity born of desperation. His muscles screamed in agony, sweat pouring down his face and blinding him, but he paid it no mind. The only thing that mattered was survival, the unrelenting drive to keep moving, to keep fighting, to keep the encroaching darkness at bay.

Then suddenly, as if mocking his perseverance, the door slammed shut with a deafening boom that shook the very foundations of the damaged structure. John's heart skipped a beat as fear gripped him like icy claws, rendering him immobile for a moment. It felt the darkness close in around him, suffocating and consuming his very being.

The moon's sickly glow intensified, casting twisted shadows that seemed to come alive and torment him. He could hear their wicked whispers and taunts echoing in the empty room, driving him closer to madness with each passing second. With all hope fading, John knew he had to keep fighting or risk being swallowed whole by this sinister place.

"What do you want from me?" John whispered again, his voice hoarse and ragged, barely recognizable to his ears. "Why are you doing this?"

Silence seemed to press down on John, the answer unspoken. The presence in the room loomed over him, watching and waiting for him to falter, to surrender to the all-consuming despair and hopelessness.

His hand trembled slightly as he flicked the switch, the light casting harsh shadows across the room. In its unyielding beam, the darkness retreated, but John could still sense its presence lurking in the corners.

With a determined grip, he swept the flashlight across the room, revealing peeling paint and distorted floors that seemed to evolve under the intense glare. The very essence of the house felt corrupted by the wrathful force that resided within its walls.

But John refused to be intimidated. He had faced darkness before and emerged victorious. This was just another battle, another test of his will and courage.

Taking a deep breath, he placed his flashlight on the rickety table and firmly grasped his tools once more. Neither would leave, and he was determined to see it off. Unbroken.

John's muscles strained as he swung his hammer, the sharp echo of each strike resonating through the empty rooms. The sound was determined, almost defiant, as if it were fighting that which lingered in the old house. But John refused to let it intimidate him.

With fierce green eyes and a determined grip on his hammer, he demolished the rotting boards with unyielding determination. Sweat dripped down his face, mixing with the thick layer of dust that coated everything in the old cottage.

As he worked, John's resolve only grew stronger. He knew he couldn't give up on this project, not when Vivienne was counting on him. She needed this old house fixed, made livable again. And he wouldn't let her down.

Surveying his progress, a wave of satisfaction washed over him. The once-crumbling mess of boards was replaced by gleaming cherry wood, bathed in the warm glow of lights that John had installed himself. His chest heaved with exertion, but it wasn't just physical exhaustion weighing on him. The presence still lingered, a haunting ghost watching him with malicious intent. But John refused to let it break him. "I won't let you win," he muttered through gritted teeth.

The thought of Vivienne's fear and desperation gave him renewed determination. She had come to him for help, and he would do whatever it took to keep her safe. With one final blow from his hammer, John set it down and wiped the sweat from his brow. He reached for his phone to check on Vivienne's whereabouts, and a pang of worry hit him. She had been absent all day and hadn't answered any of his calls or texts. Shoving his toolbox aside, he quickly dialled her number.

Relief flooded through him when she finally answered, her voice hushed and seemingly relieved as well. As they talked, he couldn't help but glance at the photo of his wife on his lock screen - a poignant reminder of why he was here.

Even after this small victory, John knew the true test was still to come. And he braced himself for whatever challenges may arise, determined to protect Vivienne and her home from any harm that may come their way.

CHAPTER 7

A Devastating Science

*Narrator's Note 25.38.2.5 -
It is a rare thing, that
which should stay buried.*

The old, creaky doors of the library protested as Vivienne stepped into the murky, amber-hued interior. Dust motes swirled and danced in the shafts of fading sunlight that slanted through arched windows, casting a warm glow over the shelves and cluttered desks. Her footsteps echoed hollowly off the dark mahogany floorboards as she strode towards the research section at the rear, shoulders hunched in determination.

Vivienne's emerald eyes scanned the towering shelves, crammed with tomes bound in cracked leather and faded cloth. Her slender fingers trailed along their spines, disturbing the patina of disuse and leaving behind traces of dust on her fingertips. Weathered gold lettering spelling out esoteric titles flashed beneath her touch -- "Compendium of Supernatural Lore," "The Phantasmagoria," "Tales from the Ethereal Realm." Yet still, the book she sought eluded her, like a hidden treasure buried among forgotten relics.

A sigh escaped her lips, scarcely louder than the whisper of yellowed pages turning in a gentle breeze. The emptiness of the library settled upon her like dust. If only John were here, his tall and sturdy frame reassuring against the shadows of doubt and dread. But he remained at Reapers Cottage, tirelessly working and sacrificing himself for their cause.

Vivienne's own pain paled in comparison to the loss that hung over Reapers Cottage like a heavy pall. Despite this, she was determined to find answers, to cling to any shred of purpose or hope that she could uncover within these hallowed walls.

Her gaze alighted on a slim volume, its fraying spine declaring "Unsolved Cases of the Moors." With trembling fingers, she plucked it from the shelf and opened it to the table of contents. There, inscribed in spidery script -- "The Haunting of Reapers Cottage." Her heart stuttered, a wild bird beating against the cage of her ribs.

At last, a sign, a glimmer of truth amidst the shadows of rumour and conjecture. Vivienne hugged the book to her chest, a talisman against the rising tide of trepidation. Every answer lay balanced on the knife's edge between revelation and regret. But she had come too far to turn back now. With a deep breath, she sank into a tattered armchair and began to read, the library's gloom gathering close like a legion of pensive spectres.

As Vivienne delved deeper into the yellowed pages, a headline caught her eye, stark and unforgiving: "Unsolved Murder Shocks Skinningrove Village." The date was smudged, the ink faded by the relentless march of time, but the words remained, a silent testament to a tragedy long buried.

With trembling hands, Vivienne gingerly unfolded the brittle, yellowed newspaper clipping. The edges were crinkled and frayed, evidence of years gone by since the article had been printed. But for Vivienne, the impact was still sharp and raw.

The faded words told a gruesome tale - the murder of Emily Thompson, a young girl who had been camping at a nearby cottage when her life was brutally taken. The community had been left reeling with shock and grief, united in their outrage that the killer had not been caught even after all these years.

As she read on, Vivienne's heart raced with emotion. Every word, every detail seemed to come alive in her mind. She could almost feel the pain and fear that must have consumed Emily in her final moments. The photos from the crime scene only added to the intensity of her emotions, the victim's vacant eyes haunting her every thought. Vivienne felt a deep sense of connection to the lost girl, their shared sorrow bonding them together.

Tears streamed down her face as she continued reading, unable to look away from the tragedy unfolding before her. In the grand scheme of things, Vivienne realised that her problems were just a drop in an ocean of human suffering.

Vivienne's heart felt heavy as she gently folded the yellowed newspaper article, her fingertips tracing over the faded headline as if seeking solace. She couldn't shake off the feeling that this discovery was only the beginning, that there was more to be uncovered in Skinningrove's dark history.

With a certainty that surpassed logic, she knew that the truth lay buried deep within the annals of this town, waiting for someone brave enough to unearth it. As she rose from the armchair, the old book clutched tightly against her chest like a precious treasure, she checked it out in silence and carefully placed it in her bag.

Vivienne's footsteps reverberated through the empty corridors of the library, adding an eerie echo to her journey toward the exit. The weight of her newfound knowledge pressed down on her shoulders like a physical burden, making each step feel heavier than the last. The once comforting silence now felt suffocating, as if the walls were listening, urging her to unravel its mysteries.

Lost in thought, she nearly collided with the frail librarian, who regarded her with a knowing look. "Find what you were looking for, dear?" the old woman asked, her voice papery.

Vivienne hesitated, the truth caught in her throat. "I... I think so," she managed, her words sounding weak and uncertain even to her ears. "But I fear it may have raised more questions than answers."

The librarian nodded, a flicker of understanding in her rheumy eyes. "The past has a way of doing that, my dear. But take heart -- the truth, however painful, is always worth pursuing."

With a murmured thanks, Vivienne stepped out into the gathering dusk, the cool evening air a welcome respite from the suffocating atmosphere of the library. As she made her way back to the cottage, her mind churned with the implications of her discovery, the pieces of the puzzle slowly falling into place.

A sharp ringing startled her out of her musings.

"John, how are you?" She answered, a warmth clambering into her voice.

"Good... I just... I've finished your flooring... and having been here all day I... was concerned I hadn't seen you..." Vivienne could hear him thinking through the phone.

"Oh I am so sorry I just got engrossed in what I was doing, I hadn't even realised the time... wait, you've finished the flooring?" Confusion washed over her.

"Yeah!" John replied excitedly, "Done it in a nice cherry wood, I think you'll like it."

"But I haven't given you the money for all the materials," Vivienne panicked, searching for her purse - she would need to get more cash out of the ATM.

"No need to worry about that, it's what I had left over, consider it my housewarming gift."

"You didn't need to do that, you're so unspeakably kind," Vivienne's face softened.

"Not at all... listen... is something going on with the cottage?" John enquired and Vivienne could sense his apprehension.

"What kind of something?" she replied, desperate not to let on, "Everything's been fine."

"Oh nothing, it was just... honestly it's nothing... forget I said anything."

A thick layer of guilt coated Vivienne's mind. She knew she should say something, but it did not do to dwell on madness.

"See you tomorrow?" He asked, his tone betraying a hope she was blind to.

"See you tomorrow, and thank you," She hung up the phone before he could respond, her social battery down to its last dregs.

As the sun set behind the misty hills, Reapers Cottage emerged from the shadows like a foreboding sentinel. The crumbling stone walls and darkened windows seemed to leer at Vivienne, daring her to enter. Her hand shook as she grasped the rusted doorknob, its icy chill seeping into her skin.

With trembling determination, she crossed inside the cottage, the musty smell of decay invading her senses. She knew that within these walls lay the secrets of Emily Thompson's murder – a case that had haunted her for months.

As she made her way through the creaking halls, her footsteps echoing ominously, she couldn't shake the feeling of being watched. And when she finally reached the room where Emily's lifeless body was found, a chill ran down her spine. For she knew that in this room, fate and death would converge once again, and she was now a part of it all.

With hesitant steps, Vivienne entered the cottage, the creaking floorboards betraying her movements. She followed the familiar path to the living room, her eyes fixated on the treasured book and photograph of Emily clutched tightly in her trembling hand. As she settled onto the faded sofa, Vivienne's mind raced with a flurry of thoughts and emotions, each one a piece of the puzzle that slowly revealed the truth.

The image of Emily's innocent smile seemed to mock her from within the confines of the aged photo, a haunting reminder of the injustice that befell the girl. The soft pink silk scarf delicately draped around her neck only added to her ethereal beauty. Vivienne's heart ached for the lost girl, her empathy pouring out with every tear that fell from her eyes.

"I'm so sorry, Emily," she whispered, "I promise I'll find out what happened to you. I won't let your story be forgotten."

A gust of wind rattled the windows with a sharp, eerie howl. Vivienne jumped in her seat, feeling a chill run down her spine. She scanned the dimly lit room, searching for any signs of a ghostly presence. But the cottage remained still, the only sound coming from the pounding of her own heart in her ears. She took a shaky breath, trying to calm her frayed nerves.

The window, already cracked from previous encounters, bowed under the pressure and cracked anew. Vivienne cursed inwardly, knowing that she would have to replace it yet again. Suddenly, an ominous face materialised on the wall. Except this time, it wasn't just on the wall. The creature sat in a rocking chair across from her, its black scales glittering in the dark. Its slit pupils widened as it realised it was being observed.

Vivienne was frozen in place, unable to tear her eyes away from the mysterious creature in front of her. The wind blew through the room again, causing her eyes to water and forcing a blink. And just like that, the creature was gone, leaving an imprint of its melancholic face burned into the wooden chair like a brand.

The warning from the librarian echoed in Vivienne's mind as she gathered her notes and clippings, her hands trembling slightly.

"Many have tried before you, my dear. But the secrets of this cottage are best left buried. No good can come from stirring up the ghosts of the past."

Vivienne stopped abruptly, feeling the beast's presence. It shook its head, a mixture of pity and resignation etched upon its weathered face.

Vivienne met its gaze, her brown eyes filled with a fierce determination. "I'm not afraid of ghosts," she said, though the quaver in her voice betrayed her true feelings. "I've faced worse in my life."

The sound of her footsteps rang through the empty, dimly lit room as she fled in a panic. Her heart pounded in her chest and her hands shook as she reached for the doorknob to her bedroom. She slammed the door shut behind her, gasping for breath as she leaned against it.

The hair on her neck stood up as she thought about what could be lurking in the shadows outside her door. Was Emily's killer still hunting for victims? Or was it something even more terrifying that had taken Emily's life and now sought to claim hers? A gust of wind rattled the windows and she shivered, pulling her cardigan tighter around her trembling body.

With cautious steps, she ventured back into the living room, which now felt eerily still and lifeless after the recent encounter. Whatever that thing was, it had disappeared for now. But she couldn't shake off the feeling that it was still watching her from afar, waiting for its next chance to strike.

She carefully set her worn leather-bound notes down on the battered, mahogany coffee table before sinking into the sofa. Her mind buzzed with the implications of what she had just discovered. The sepia-toned photograph of Emily, the woman whose mysterious disappearance had haunted her for years, stared up at her from the table. The intensity of those haunting eyes seemed to bore into Vivienne's brain like a sharp drill.

Desperate to block out the unsettling images that flashed through her mind, Vivienne closed her eyes and took a deep breath. But it was futile. The darkness, creeping in since she found the shocking truth, had consumed her completely, and there was no turning back now.

As dusk settled in and shadows stretched across the room, Vivienne sat alone in her quaint cottage, her thoughts spiralling out of control. She could feel a presence in the room with her, a faint whisper at the edge of her consciousness, watching and waiting to strike.

In a moment of madness, an idea gripped her mind, and refused to let go. She needed to speak to Emily.

Her hands trembling with anticipation, Vivienne arranged seven candles in a perfect circle around her, their flickering flames casting eerie dancing shadows on the walls of the living room. The air grew thick with a heady mix of scents - melting wax and heavy perfume - as she lit each candle with a single match. Finally, she placed the faded photograph of Emily at the circle's centre, its cracked surface reflecting the flickering light. The young girl's frozen gaze seemed to pierce through the veil of time and space, beckoning Vivienne closer into the unknown depths of her mind.

"Emily," Vivienne whispered, her voice quivering. "If you can hear me, please give me a sign. Help me understand what happened to you."

Vivienne's body tensed as she sat cross-legged on the hardwood floor, surrounded by a circle of lit candles. She could hear her rapid breathing and the ticking of the antique clock on the mantel. With trembling hands, she placed them on top of an Ouija board and closed her eyes.

The silence in the dimly lit cottage was thick and heavy, like a blanket suffocating her. Vivienne focused all her energy on connecting with the spirit world, desperate to make contact with the murdered girl whose restless soul haunted these walls.

Minutes dragged by, each one feeling like an eternity. Doubts and fears crept into Vivienne's mind, questioning her sanity and beliefs. But just as she was about to give up hope, a sudden gust of wind swept through the room, extinguishing some of the candles and causing the remaining ones to flicker wildly.

Vivienne's eyes snapped open, her heart pounding against her ribcage. She scanned the room, searching for any sign of a ghostly presence. Her senses were on high alert, but all she could feel was the mocking emptiness of the cottage.

"Please, Emily," Vivienne pleaded, tears stinging her eyes. "I want to help you. I need to know the truth."

As the words left her lips, a powerful gust of wind erupted in the room, snuffing out the final flickers of candlelight and plunging the cottage into pitch-black darkness. Vivienne's heart raced as she let out a terrified scream, her hands flailing wildly in search of the matches that seemed to have vanished into thin air.

But just as she was about to give up hope, a sinister whisper pierced through the silence, a haunting voice that seemed to surround her from every direction. Vivienne's blood ran cold as she froze in fear, straining to decipher the cryptic words that echoed through the air.

"Help me," the voice whispered, filled with anguish and despair. "Please, help me."

Vivienne's mind reeled with the implications of what she had just heard. Was it truly the spirit of Emily, reaching out from beyond the grave? Or was it something else entirely, the bold entity that sat in her rocking chair mere hours ago?

As she sat in the darkness, surrounded by the echoes of the past, Vivienne knew that she had no choice but to press on. For the sake of Emily's soul, and the sake of her sanity, she would stop at nothing to uncover the truth behind the young girl's murder.

Even if it meant facing the demons that lurked within the shadows of the cottage, waiting to claim her as their own.

Vivienne's voice trembled as she called out into the darkness, her words a desperate plea for understanding. "Emily, if that's you, please give me a sign. I'm here to help you, to find out what happened to you."

Vivienne's tense body remained still, her breathing shallow and eyes wide as she waited for any sign of the restless spirit. The air was thick with anticipation, charged with the potential of a supernatural encounter.

Suddenly, a cold breeze swept across the back of her neck like icy fingers, causing goosebumps to rise on her skin. A shiver ran down her spine as she whirled around, searching desperately for any sign of the presence lurking in the shadows.

"Emily?" Vivienne called out, her voice quivering with fear and uncertainty. But there was no answer, only the creaking of old floorboards beneath her feet.

Then, like a haunting response to her call, a soft, mournful sob reverberated through the room. The sound seemed to carry with it all the pain and sorrow of a life tragically cut short. Vivienne's heart tightened with empathy for the young girl, for the injustice of her death and the unresolved mystery that surrounded it.

"I won't let them forget you, Emily," Vivienne vowed, her voice growing stronger with each word. "I'll find out who did this to you, and I'll make sure they pay for what they've done."

A solemn promise that Vivienne knew she would stop at nothing to keep. Even if it meant delving into the darkest corners of the human soul, even if it meant confronting the ghosts of her troubled past.

With a determined hand, Vivienne reached for the matches, feeling their rough wooden texture beneath her fingertips. She was ready to reignite the flames of her investigation, to embark on a journey that would lead her towards the truth. And she would not rest until she had brought it to light, no matter the cost.

As the match sparked and ignited, the sudden flare of light that filled the room was blinding. It seemed as if every corner of the room was illuminated, casting shadows that twisted and contorted like living creatures. The air grew cold with inhumanity, the essence of Emily's spirit had permeated the space, demanding to be heard.

Objects began to rattle and shake, their movements erratic and violent, as if propelled by an unseen force. Books flew from their shelves, pages fluttering like wounded birds before crashing to the floor in a chaotic frenzy. Pictures trembled on their hooks before falling with a resounding thud, their glass frames shattering into countless glittering shards that scattered across the room like fallen stars.

Vivienne's heart raced, her breath coming in short, panicked gasps as the walls seemed to close in around her, the room shrinking with each passing second. She could feel the weight of rage bearing down upon her, a suffocating force that threatened to consume her entirely.

"Emily, please!" Vivienne cried out, her voice trembling with fear and desperation. "I'm trying to help you! I want to find out what happened to you, to bring you the justice you deserve!"

The spirit's fury raged on, the foundations of the cottage were being torn apart. Vivienne stumbled backward, her hands frantically searching for something to hold onto as the room seemed to spin and sway around her.

Fear crawled up her spine, but she refused to give in to it. Determination burned fiercely within her, pushing her to stand her ground against the overwhelming force before her. Her mind was a whirlwind of conflicting emotions - terror, anger, sadness - all battling for control over her thoughts. She knew that to flee now would mean abandoning Emily's spirit to an eternity of restless wandering, trapped in the very place where she had met her tragic end. The cottage's walls trembled, and Vivienne could almost feel the weight of Emily's presence.

With a herculean effort, Vivienne forced herself to stand tall, her voice ringing loud and clear above the noise. "Enough!"

Vivienne stood like a solitary figure in the centre of the room, her declaration in the air like a dark cloud. The frenzied activity that had filled the room just moments before came to an abrupt halt, leaving an unnatural silence that seemed to seep into Vivienne's being and fill her with unease. She scanned the shadows, her eyes darting from one corner to another, searching for any sign of what was to come. Her heart raced, each beat echoing through the night's stillness.

And then, a faint whisper broke through the quiet - a chilling voice calling out for help, barely audible but carrying a desperate plea for salvation. Vivienne's breath caught in her throat as she realised her request had been granted.

With determination and fear warring within her, Vivienne slowly retreated from the living room, her feet making soft thuds on the singing wooden floorboards. She made her way up the dark staircase, every step bringing her closer to her bedroom where she hoped to find some respite from the sapping presence.

CHAPTER 8

Sleep, Sweetie

Narrator's Note 19.13.2.11 - No journey should be undertaken alone.

Each step John took on the gravel path towards the weathered cottage was like a heavy burden, the sound loud and jarring in the stillness of the countryside. The cracked and peeling façade of the cottage seemed to welcome him, a familiar sight in this desolate landscape. Through the single window, a burst of vibrant colour caught his eye, a testament to Vivienne's presence in the once-abandoned place.

As he drew nearer, the cottage's door flowed open, revealing Vivienne's hauntingly beautiful face. Her once lively eyes now shone with a desperate hope, a glimmer of light in the darkness surrounding her. "John," she breathed, her voice carrying on the mournful wind like a delicate song. "You came."

John nodded solemnly, his usually strong voice now soft and filled with unspoken sorrow. "I couldn't stay away." He gazed upon Vivienne, taking in the toll time apart had taken on her petite features.

Vivienne stepped aside, beckoning him into the cottage with a trembling hand. "Please, come inside. There is so much I need to share with you, so much we need to uncover." Her words were urgent, pleading for understanding and closure as they both struggled to make sense of their past and find a way forward.

Vivienne beckoned John to follow her deeper into the dimly lit cottage, their movements echoing off walls. The air was thick and musty, carrying an ominous aura that made John's skin crawl. His mind raced with the implications of what lay ahead, his heart pounding in his chest.

As they entered the living room, John's eyes took in the worn-out furniture and faded decor. The once vibrant colours now drained of life, leaving behind a hollow shell of a home. Vivienne's voice trembled, adding a mournful backdrop to the disquiet.

"I've gathered everything I could find," Vivienne said, gesturing to the cluttered coffee table. A scattered array of newspaper clippings, photographs, and handwritten notes covered its surface, a tangible representation of her relentless pursuit for answers.

John's heart sank as Vivienne admitted to lying about the state of the cottage. He couldn't deny the strange occurrences he had experienced here, but it was comforting to know he wasn't alone in his experiences. "What is it?" he asked, bracing himself for her answer.

Vivienne fidgeted compulsively before speaking again. "Something not of this world," she whispered, sending shivers down John's spine. He couldn't help but feel a sense of dread at her words and wondered what other secrets this old cottage held within its walls.

"I went to the library when you were here doing my floor, and I think it's Emily trying to make contact."

Vivienne's hands trembled as she gingerly picked up the stack of papers, her eyes darting with feverish intensity from one piece to the next. It was like searching for a needle in a haystack, trying to find some hidden pattern amidst the chaos and confusion. John watched on, his heart pounding with equal parts anticipation and dread, bracing himself for whatever revelations lay ahead.

As they delved deeper into the evidence, the unsolved case lay upon them like a sea fret, suffocating and relentless. It felt like an inescapable voyeur, threatening to consume them both. For John, there was also the familiar knot of guilt that tightened in his chest. Together, they might finally unravel the dark secrets that had haunted them for so long.

Vivienne's voice shook as she recounted the grisly details of the murder, her words interrupted by occasional sniffling sobs.

"She was found in the cottage," she began haltingly. "Her body...it was brutalized beyond recognition."

John winced at the memory of those crime scene photos; it was an image that would never leave him.

"The police deemed it the work of a madman," Vivienne continued, her voice growing stronger with conviction. "But I can't shake this feeling that there's more to the story. Something they overlooked."

John listened intently, his mind immediately flooded with memories of the case that had consumed him for years. The sleepless nights spent pouring over evidence and leads, only to hit constant dead ends. The frustration and self-doubt that came with being unable to bring closure to the victim's family. As Vivienne spoke, he couldn't help but feel a pang of regret and remorse, wondering if he could have done more.

"I've tried to find answers," Vivienne continued, her voice barely above a whisper. "But I've hit a wall. I know I've no right to ask anything of you at all, you've already been way too kind, but what do you think?"

John's head bobbed in silent agreement, his gaze unwavering as he stared at the pictures scattered before him. The images, though grainy and faded, still held a chilling power that sent shivers down his spine. Each one was a haunting reminder of the brutal and senseless crime that had taken place. With trembling fingers, he traced the edges of the photographs, feeling the weight of pain and suffering contained within them seep into his very being.

"I should have done more," he murmured, his voice heavy with guilt. "I was the lead detective on the case, and I let it go cold. I let the killer slip away, and I let the family down. I'll never forgive myself for that."

"I had no idea you were involved in the case," Vivienne stood still for a moment, as if surveying him. She reached out and placed a hand on his arm, her touch gentle and reassuring. "You did everything you could, John. You can't blame yourself for the actions of a monster."

But even as she spoke the words, John could see the doubt in her eyes, the unspoken question that lingered between them. Had he truly done everything in his power to bring the killer to justice, or had he allowed his weakness and failings to stand in the way?

"You truly had no idea this was my case? Or do you mean to taunt me?" John bit out, his guilt reshaping itself into anger. As he glanced back at her eyes, now welling with tears, he felt her withdraw. Any part of him that thought she was rubbing salt into a wound disappeared instantly.

"Sorry," He managed, rolling his head in his hands.

John's shoulders sagged, his eyes fixed on the worn floorboards beneath his feet. The silence stretched between them, heavy with the unspoken pain of the past. Finally, he lifted his gaze to meet Vivienne's, his green eyes restless.

"I've carried this guilt with me for so long," he whispered, his deep voice cracking with emotion. "It's eaten away at me, day after day, year after year. I've tried to bury it, to push it down and pretend it does not exist, but it's always there, lurking."

Vivienne's hand tightened on his arm, her touch a lifeline in the darkness of his despair. "You can't keep punishing yourself, John. You did everything you could with the evidence you had. Sometimes, no matter how hard we try, justice eludes us."

John shook his head, a bitter laugh escaping his lips. "Justice? What justice is there in a world where a killer can walk free while an innocent life is cut short? What justice is there in a world where a family is left to mourn, forever wondering why their loved one was taken from them?"

He rose to his feet, his tall frame casting long shadows across the room. He paced back and forth, his footsteps heavy on the creaking floorboards. "I became a detective to help people, to bring closure and peace to those who needed it most. But in the end, I couldn't even do that. I failed them, Vivienne. I failed them all."

Vivienne stood and crossed the room to him, her hand reaching up shakily to cup his stubbled cheek. "You didn't fail them, John. You could have walked out of here as soon as I brought it up. You didn't. That takes courage and strength, more than most people possess. You may not have been able to bring the killer to justice then, but you can still honour the victim's memory by seeking the truth now."

John leaned into her touch, his eyes fluttering closed as he inhaled deeply. The delicate scent of her perfume enveloped him, a pleasant mix of blooming roses and warm vanilla. For a brief moment, he was transported to a world where his past didn't exist, and hope for a brighter future filled his heart. In that fleeting instant, he allowed himself to imagine rewriting the mistakes of yesterday and carving out a new path for himself. The darkness that threatened to consume him receded, replaced by the warmth and comfort of her embrace.

Vivienne slowly pulled her hand away, unsure of what to make of the intense connection they had just shared. For a brief moment, he was lost in her and the warmth of her touch. But as he regained his senses, he couldn't help but feel a tinge of unease settle over him. This was not how things were supposed to be, and reality came crashing down like an avalanche on a fragile roof.

"I don't know if I can do this," John pulled at his shirt, everything in and around his body stifling him.

Vivienne's gaze held his, unwavering in its intensity. "You won't fail, John. We'll do this together. Your experience as a detective and my research skills - we'll make a formidable team. I foresee great things well beyond these four walls for you."

John nodded slowly, his lips betraying a small smile as he registered his own words being quoted back to him, his resolve strengthening with each passing second. He reached out and took Vivienne's hand in his, craving the softness of her skin against his calloused palm. "You're right," he said, his voice steady now.

Vivienne swallowed hard, her hand felt captured, compromised.

Vivienne smiled then, a radiant beam of light amidst the gloom of the cottage. "Together, we'll find a way," she said, her words a solemn vow. "We'll follow every lead, chase down every clue until we unravel the mystery that has haunted us both."

As they stood there, hand in hand, John felt a sense of purpose wash over him, a clarity of mind that had eluded him for years.

With a final, determined nod, John stood tall and threw their belongings into black leather bags. Vivienne stacked folders of research, each page marked with handwritten notes and highlighted passages. They moved with urgency, fueled by the weight of their mission. Just as they stepped outside, a fierce wind whipped through the trees, the rustling leaves sounding like distant whispers. The darkness of the night pressed in on them, draping over their shoulders like a heavy cloak. But they didn't falter - they were ready to face whatever lay ahead in their quest for the truth.

But as they exchanged a glance, their eyes locked in a silent promise, John felt a little taller Vivienne's presence beside him was a beacon of light, a reminder that he was no longer alone in his quest for redemption. But she would not look at him, her eyes scanning the landscape, her feet tapping between steps.

Something still hung in the air and he worried anew, that this story was only half told.

CHAPTER 9

Tuesday's Girl with the Brown Eyes

Narrator's Note 19.28.2.7 -
For every step forward,
many are taken backward,
until we learn otherwise.

John slumped in the overstuffed armchair, its once-luxurious velvet upholstery now dusty and threadbare, soaking up his tears like parched earth in a drought. His large frame seemed to shrink as he hunched over, broad shoulders caving inward under his grief. The room around him was a testament to his despair - empty whiskey bottles littered the floor like discarded memories, their dull glimmer catching the light of a single brass lamp that cast liquid shadows across his anguished face.

In John's trembling hands, he held a framed photograph of Odelia - her ethereal beauty captured forever behind the glass. Her flaxen tresses spilled down her porcelain shoulders, framing her rosebud lips frozen in an enigmatic Mona Lisa smile. But it was her sparkling ocean eyes that caught his attention - once radiant with mirth and mischief, they now only taunted him with their forever-silenced secrets.

"Odelia..." His ragged baritone cracked as he traced a trembling finger over her beloved face. "My darling Odelia..." Sobs wracked his body, spilling fresh rivulets down grizzled cheeks.

Memories danced unbidden through his tortured mind - the musical chime of her aristocratic laugh echoing in golden summer fields, the sensual whisper of lace against bare skin in their marital bed, heated words, and icy silences in those final dark days. If only he could have saved her, sheltered her fragile soul from the cruel winds of fate. What good was all his strength, his wealth, his cunning, if he couldn't protect what mattered most?

"Forgive me, my love," he rasped, pressing trembling lips to her photographed ones. "Forgive me." The penance of a sinner to his spectral saint, an unbreakable vow whispered to unfeeling glass. He cradled her portrait to his chest as if he could absorb her essence through osmosis and resuscitate her with the sheer force of his yearning.

But Odelia remained still and silent, forever imprisoned behind her gilded frame, forever lost to him in this mortal coil.

And John wept, adrift in an ocean of misery, drowning in the bitter dregs of memory and regret. Without her, he was a haunted husk of a man, a wraith wandering the bleak moors of his mind. How could he go on, when all the light had been leached from his world?

Yet even as despair threatened to consume him, a tiny ember of resolve flickered in his broken heart. Odelia had been his guiding star, his true north - and though her earthly light had been extinguished, he knew she would want him to persevere. To seek justice, redemption, and perhaps even a reason to live again. He owed her that much.

John pressed a final reverent kiss to her portrait before laying it gently aside. Then he heaved himself to his feet, swaying slightly as the ocean of whiskey sloshed in his veins. Grabbing a half-empty bottle, he raised it heavenward.

"To you, my darling," he declared, his voice a low, gravelly rumble. "Until we meet again, in this world or the next." He knocked back a long pull, relishing the slow burn down his throat. Then he staggered towards the door, ready to face the demons that howled beyond.

The unsolved murder case - and Odelia's loss - gnawed at his very soul, an inescapable torment that haunted his every waking moment.

John sat in his dimly lit apartment, surrounded by empty bottles of whiskey and the remnants of a shattered picture frame. Odelia's hauntingly beautiful face, now marred by cracks, stared back at him from the remaining fragments.

As the weight of her loss crushed him once again, John let out a guttural cry that echoed through the lonely walls. He gripped his hair in frustration, his fingers tangling in the unruly strands as he screamed her name into the darkness. Tears streamed down his face, mingling with the taste of alcohol on his lips.

"Why?" he pleaded to the empty room. "How could you leave me?" His trembling hand reached for another bottle but instead found a sharp piece of glass on the floor. He picked it up, watching as the light reflected off its edges and cast a crimson hue onto his skin.

Suddenly, he was filled with rage and sorrow all at once. With a primal roar, he threw the shard across the room, sending it crashing into the wall. He collapsed onto the floor amidst the scattered shards and broken memories, his body wracked with sobs.

But in that moment of utter despair, John felt a brief glimmer of hope. He remembered Odelia's unwavering belief in him, her love that had always lifted him up even in his darkest moments. With renewed determination, he wiped away his tears and stood up.

Even as he felt his heart bleeding from the wound caused by the shattered glass, John knew that Odelia's love would forever be etched into his soul.

"I will find them, my love," he whispered, his voice a solemn vow.

He closed his eyes, allowing himself one last moment to dwell in the bittersweet memories of their life together. Sunlight filtered through the window, casting a golden glow on the shattered shards of glass that littered the floor like scattered jewels. With a short breath, he rose to his feet, the broken pieces crunching beneath his boots as he strode towards the door, a man on a mission.

Driven by an unquenchable thirst for destruction that now consumed him, John staggered across the room. His hand outstretched, desperately grasping for the half-empty bottle of whiskey that stood like a beacon of false hope amidst the chaos. His fingers curled around the cool glass, the amber liquid sloshing within as he brought it to his lips with a trembling hand. The whiskey burned his throat, a familiar sensation that offered a fleeting moment of warmth in the cold, unforgiving emptiness that had become his constant companion.

But as the alcohol coursed through his veins, the room began to spin. The once-familiar walls morphed into a twisted, nightmarish landscape. Patterns seemed to dance and writhe, their movements mocking his pain. Their whispers echoed in his ears like taunts from beyond the grave. John's grief, a tangible entity, wrapped itself around him like tissue round bone, dragging him deeper into the abyss of his despair.

The deafening silence that followed was a harsh reminder of the void that Odelia's absence had left in John's life. His legs gave way beneath him, and he collapsed to the floor, the bottle slipping from his trembling fingers and shattering against the polished hardwood. The shards of glass glinted in the dim light, each a cruel reflection of the jagged pieces of his broken heart.

As he knelt amidst the wreckage of his life, John's mind began to wander, drifting to the darkest corners of his psyche. The lines between reality and nightmare blurred, and for a fleeting moment, he could have sworn he felt Odelia's presence. He could almost feel her ghostly fingers brush against his cheek in a gesture of comfort. But when he reached out to touch her, his hand met only empty air, a bitter reminder of the cruel trick his mind had played.

John's fists clenched, his knuckles turning white as he fought to hold back the guttural scream threatening to escape his throat. Memories assaulted him with relentless force, each one a twisted knife piercing through his shattered heart. He saw Odelia's lifeless body, her once beautiful skin now marked by the noose that had taken her away from him. Her vibrant eyes were now dull and empty, a haunting sight that would forever torment him. The weight of guilt pressed down upon him like a heavy stone, crushing him beneath its unforgiving mass as he conceded he had failed to protect her from the darkness that consumed her.

His sobs trailed in the air, weaving that which threatened to suffocate him. The silence of the room felt like a touchable thing, pressing against his chest and squeezing out any hope or comfort. John's guilt was an insidious creature, coiled tightly around his heart and crushing it with every laboured breath. It was a constant reminder of his failures, his obsession with solving cold cases overshadowing everything else in his life.

But as he sat there, drowning in self-pity and regret, it suddenly hit him like a ton of bricks. He had been so consumed by his own pain that he had failed to see the cracks in Odelia's façade, the silent cries for help that she had been sending out for months. With a roar of anguish, John surged to his feet, fists slamming against the wall with a sickening crack. The physical pain that shot through his hands was nothing compared to the overwhelming agony that consumed his soul. But for a brief moment, it provided a welcome distraction from the all-encompassing grief and guilt.

John let out a primal howl of rage and despair that echoed through the empty house like a mournful dirge, one the walls had heard often enough. It was a sound born from the very depths of his being, a manifestation of all the pain and anguish he had bottled up inside for far too long. And in that fleeting moment, as his screams filled the air, John allowed the guilt to subside to feel fully – pure, unadulterated sorrow.

"I'm sorry, Odelia," he sobbed, his forehead pressed against the cool plaster of the wall. "I'm so sorry."

As John's knees buckled beneath him, his body crumpling to the floor in a heap of despair, a faint whisper echoed through the room, a voice that was both familiar and foreign, a ghostly melody that pierced through the veil of his grief.

"John, my love," the voice murmured, a gentle caress that seemed to emanate from the very air around him. "You must not do this. This is not you."

John's heart stuttered in his chest, his breath catching in his throat as he recognized the lilting cadence of Odelia's voice, that had always sent shivers down his spine. He lifted his head, his eyes searching the room for any sign of her presence, desperate to catch a glimpse of the woman he had loved more than life itself.

"Odelia?" he croaked, his voice barely above a whisper. "Is that really you?"

There was a moment of silence, a pause that stretched on for an eternity, before the voice spoke again, this time with a hint of amusement. "Of course it's me, darling. Who else would bother to haunt you in your darkest hour?"

Despite the heaviness in his heart, John felt a flicker of a smile tug at the corners of his mouth, a brief respite from the unrelenting sorrow that had consumed him. "I thought I'd lost you forever," he confessed, his voice breaking on the last word.

"You could never lose me, John," Odelia replied, her words a soothing balm to his battered soul. "But this brooding, this lashing out... it has to stop. You are not this broken thing incapable of getting up off your knees."

John closed his eyes, his breath shuddering in his chest as he fought back the tears that threatened to overwhelm him once more. He knew that Odelia was right, that he couldn't allow himself to be consumed by his grief, to let it destroy him from the inside out. But the thought of moving on without her, of facing the world alone, was almost more than he could bear.

"I suppose you think me frightfully cliche.." John chuckled, heartened to hear Odelia laugh in response.

"Indeed, but I married the walking cliche so I guess that's on me." She winked at him, her soft smile betraying an easy familiarity.

With a trembling hand, John reached out, his fingers grazing the shattered remnants of the photograph scattered across the floor. Each jagged piece was a reminder of the life he had lost, the love that had been ripped away from him in the cruellest of ways. But as he stared at the broken glass, he realised that he too was shattered, his very soul torn asunder by the weight of his grief.

"I don't know if I can do this without you," he whispered, his voice raw. "I don't know if I have the strength to go on."

Odelia's ghostly form shimmered before him. "You are stronger than you know, John," she said, her voice firm but gentle. "You have always been the rock that others have clung to in times of crisis, I have seen you become that again over recent days. Now it is time for you to be your own anchor, to find your way."

"I will try," he said, his voice hoarse. "For you, my love."

Odelia smiled. "Good, and unless you're putting on a shit, edgy theatre version of Ten Green Bottles, I suggest you deal with those." She pointed at the empty whiskey bottles, before placing the gentlest of kisses on his forehead.

With a final, lingering look at the spectral form of his beloved wife, John turned towards the door, empty bottles in hand to bin, his steps heavy but determined.

As he reached for the doorknob, John paused, his hand trembling slightly. He knew that once he stepped through that door, there would be no turning back, no retreating into the numbing embrace of alcohol and despair.

With a deep breath, John turned the knob and stepped out into the hallway, ready to face whatever lay ahead.

CHAPTER 10

Life on a Landslide

Narrator's Note 3.27.6.11 - Some decisions are made in the same way a heart attack comes on, all of a sudden, and the outcome is often the same.

Vivienne's footsteps echoed against the floorboards, her agitation growing with each back-and-forth pace. The fading afternoon light filtered through the old windows, casting long shadows that danced along the walls. She couldn't help but glance at her wristwatch for what felt like the hundredth time, anxiety bubbling up in her stomach with each passing minute. John should have arrived by now to help with the renovations, just as they had planned. But his absence felt like a gaping void, growing colder and darker by the minute.

Feeling restless and alone, Vivienne wandered into the rustic kitchen, where an old wooden table sat near a window overlooking the overgrown garden. She absentmindedly picked up her mobile phone from the counter, fingers trembling slightly as she dialled John's number. With each unanswered ring, her heart sank deeper and deeper. It was almost as if the silence was mocking her, emphasising her isolation and helplessness. Finally, the call went to voicemail, John's deep voice no longer a comforting presence but an unreachable comfort in her mind.

"John, it's me...Vivienne," she said softly, her words echoing in the stillness of the cottage. "I thought we were supposed to meet today to work on the renovations. Is everything alright? Please...call me back when you can."

Vivienne set the phone down with a heavy thud, a wave of guilt and self-doubt crashing over her like a relentless tide. She could feel it on her, suffocating and consuming. Had she misunderstood their plans, or had John simply forgotten? A chill ran through her at the thought of him purposely choosing not to come, finding her company a burden amid his own grief.

Seeking solace from the suffocating emotions swirling within her, Vivienne moved to the living room window. She gazed out at the overgrown garden, its once-tamed beauty now a wild reflection of her inner turmoil. The fading light cast an ethereal glow upon the wilting flowers and twisting vines, adding a haunting quality to the scene. It was a reminder of the impermanence of life, a stark contrast to the memories of happier times that flooded Vivienne's mind - when this very cottage had been filled with if not joy then contentment.

As the sun dipped out, darkness crept in around Vivienne like a cloud. She sank into the worn armchair, her eyes fixed on the silent phone as if willing it to ring with news of John's whereabouts. But there was no sound, no indication that he was thinking of her. As she sat there, strands of hair stuck to her tear-stained cheeks. The room was silent except for the faint sound of her uneven breathing. Above her, a crack in the ceiling seemed to mock her, reminding her of everything she had tried and failed at. She pulled a blanket tighter around herself, feeling chained by the weight of loneliness that seemed to crush her chest.

Vivienne sat on the edge of her chair, fidgeting with the hem of her blanket as she stared at the empty space beside her.

She couldn't shake off the guilt that had consumed her since John left. Her puffy, water-logged eyes mirrored the dark, stormy clouds outside her window. She wondered if her struggles had been too much for him to handle, if her brokenness had finally pushed him away. The silence in the room was palpable, a constant reminder of his absence as she spiralled further and further down.

She sat still as stone, her eyes trained on the looming shapes in the corners. The space where John used to sit was now filled with an eerie silence, a constant reminder of the emptiness that consumed her heart.

With great effort, Vivienne pushed herself out of the armchair, every movement like wading through thick tar. She shuffled towards the window, drawn to the expansive darkness beyond the glass. The night stretched before her like a never-ending abyss, a deep well of nothing. Even the stars seemed to have abandoned her, hidden behind a veil of black clouds.

"What have I done?" she whispered, her voice like a knife through flesh. "Why must I be like this?"

As Vivienne's mind churned with self-recrimination, the unanswered questions coated the air like a thick fog. She had poured her heart and soul into this cottage, into the dream of a fresh start, but it all felt like a cruel mockery of her hopes. The walls closed in on her, sensing blood for the taking.

Her thoughts turned to the small bottle of sleeping pills hidden away in her nightstand, a secret she had kept from John. She had acquired them in a moment of weakness, a desperate attempt to find some escape from the consuming pain that haunted her every waking moment. Now, in her despair, the temptation to end it all grew stronger with each passing minute.

With heavy limbs, Vivienne made her way towards the bedroom. The creature had chanced being seen, following her intently, whispering seductively of release and oblivion. Her hand trembled as she reached for the drawer, her fingers closing around the small, innocuous bottle that held the key to her escape.

As she held the pills in her palm, a strange sense of calm washed over her. This was not how she would go out. The thought of her body being found brought an unimaginable trauma. Her eyes fixed on the shoreline and the tumultuous waves crashing down upon it. She knew now how it would end. The decision had been made, the path chosen. There was no turning back now. She returned to the table, almost on autopilot, sitting calmly.

With a shaking hand, Vivienne fumbled for a pen and paper, her vision clouded by tears that threatened to spill from her eyes. She lowered herself onto the hard wooden chair at the kitchen table, the harsh fluorescent light casting an eerie glow upon her pale and haggard face. Her heart heavy and her chest constricted, she took a painful breath and began to pour it all out onto the page in front of her. The room's inactivity was only broken by the scratching of pen on paper as she bared her soul one last time.

"My dearest John," she wrote, her hand trembling with each stroke of the pen. "I'm so sorry for the pain I'm about to cause you, but I can't go on like this any longer. I had thought to wait until the house was finished to depart this life but something has snapped and I cannot unsnap it. I know we've known each other for a matter of days, but these days I have been more cared for than the rest of my years put together. I am sorry it is you, of all people, that must receive this letter."

Vivienne's words flowed onto the paper like a torrent of anguish, her innermost thoughts and feelings laid bare in stark, unrelenting prose.

"I know you'll blame yourself for this," she continued, her hand shaking so violently that she could barely keep the pen steady. "But please, don't. This is my choice, my burden to bear. You have given me more compassion than I ever thought possible, but even that cannot save me from myself. It is not for you to be held captive by my insecurities."

As she wrote, Vivienne's mind was a maelstrom of emotions - sadness, guilt, and a desperate longing for release from the pain that had become her constant companion. The words seemed to blur before her eyes, the ink smudged by the tears streaming freely down her cheeks.

"I hope that someday, you'll be able to forgive me for this," she wrote, her hand hesitating for a moment as she struggled to find the right words. "I know that my actions will cause you immeasurable pain, but please know that I am doing this to free myself from this pit. The sea will take me and I will be gone, there will be nothing else to do."

Tears splattered on the paper as Vivienne scrawled her signature at the bottom of the page. She folded the note with shaking hands, ink everywhere in the process. The weight of her decision lifted slightly and her features relaxed.

In the dimly lit room, shadows melted into one another, and Vivienne sat at the table clutching the note like a lifeline. Memories of happier times mixed with an uneasy calm as she stared into the flickering candle, the memories of her past mingling with the hopelessness of her present.

"I never wanted it to come to this," her voice was almost non-existent above the howling wind. "I thought I could escape my past, start a new life... but it seems fate had other plans for me."

She closed her eyes, the tears still flowing freely down her cheeks as she pictured John's face, the concern that had always shone in his piercing green eyes now replaced by a mixture of pain and betrayal. The creases around his eyes deepened, highlighting the hurt in his expression. Vivienne could almost feel the weight of his gaze on her as she stood there with a heavy heart.

The thought of causing him such unyielding anguish tore at her heart, threatening to break it with each passing moment. She took slow, shaky breaths, trying to gather her resolve and steel herself for what was about to come. But no matter how hard she tried, she couldn't shake off the overwhelming guilt and regret that consumed her.

With a final, shuddering sigh, Vivienne rose from the table, her whole body trembling with emotion. She placed the note carefully on the table where it would be seen, feeling like she was leaving a piece of her soul behind. As she moved through the cottage like a ghost, her footsteps echoed hollowly on the wooden floors, adding to the eerie atmosphere. Each step felt like a condemnation, a reminder of the inevitable consequences of her actions.

Finally reaching the door, Vivienne turned back one last time to take in the familiar surroundings. It felt surreal to think that this place would soon only hold memories of her. Even the beast that lived in this place looked at her with a pitying smile. With a heavy heart and tear-stained face, she turned the doorknob and stepped out into the world, uncertain of what lay ahead but knowing that there was no turning back.

As her feet dragged through the thick, wet sand on the beach, grains of mud and grit clung to her skin, making her nightie stick uncomfortably. Each step was a struggle against the weight of her tired body, and her nerves were adding to the sweat that drenched her skin. She could feel every grain of sand and speck of dirt grinding into her flesh, leaving behind a trail of discomfort as she trudged on toward the shore.

"Take me," she whispered, her eyes fluttering closed as she surrendered herself to the stormy ocean, willing to be whisked away by the tide. "Let me find the peace I have been denied in this life. Let me be free."

The shadows on the beach seemed to deepen as Vivienne drifted motionless in the sea, her body weightless and vulnerable against the vast expanse of water. The gentle rhythm of the waves rocked her, their salty spray stinging her skin. Her breath came in deep, each one releasing her into the tide. She closed her eyes and let herself be carried away, waiting for the inevitable end to come. The sun had set behind the horizon, casting an eerie glow over the scene, as if nature itself was mourning her impending demise.

"I never meant to hurt anyone," she whispered, her voice drowned out by the water. "I only wanted to be loved, to exist without pain. But I see now that I am too broken, too damaged to find it all."

As she spoke, Vivienne's fingers traced the outline of a small scar on her wrist, a constant reminder of the pain and suffering that had defined her life. But then her thoughts shifted to John, who had shown her kindness and offered a glimmer of hope. She remembered how he would brush his hand against hers as they talked, a simple gesture that meant so much.

Vivienne's hand clawed at the sea, attempting to tighten around the water that now slipped through her hands. There was no going back now. She knew deep down that this was the only path left for her, and she was ready to take it head-on.

"Is this to be my final resting place?" she thought. "Will I finally find the peace I've been searching for, or will I be condemned to an eternity of suffering?"

Vivienne's mind raced with thoughts of the afterlife, of the judgement that awaited her on the other side. She had never been a religious woman, but now, faced with the prospect of her mortality, she found herself wondering if there was some truth to the stories she had heard as a child. And if so, would God be merciful? That her final thoughts would be of God, was an irony not lost upon her.

The reality of her situation was far more grim, far more final than most endings could ever be.

But as the minutes ticked by and all remained silent, Vivienne knew it was done. John was gone, and she was alone, left to face the consequences of her choices on her own.

Vivienne closed her eyes, surrendering herself to the darkness that awaited her. As she drifted off into a dreamless sleep, she could hear the whispered voice of the creature, calling out to her from the shadows, promising her the release she so desperately craved.

CHAPTER 11

Belsize Park

*Narrator's Note 21.4.6.23 -
Familiarity is often easier
than better things.*

John's grip on the whiskey bottle was loose, his fingers barely able to hold on as he slumped in the threadbare armchair. The amber liquid swirled and sloshed against the glass, a warning he chose not to take. His eyes were fixed on the dying embers in the fireplace, the light casting eerie shadows across his haggard face. Faded photographs lay scattered across the coffee table, evidence of an inevitable spiral.

A chill breeze whispered through the room, causing John to shiver and pull his coat tighter around him. But not just the cold caused his tremors - his mind was lost in the labyrinthine depths of all that had consumed him.

He lifted the bottle to his lips, desperate for its numbing effects to dull the ache in his chest. The liquid burned as it went down, but it was a welcome distraction from the accusing voices that haunted his every waking moment. They taunted him with endless questions and doubts, reminding him he may never find peace.

"Oh, John..." The melodic, aristocratic voice cut through the gloom, tinged with a familiar sarcasm that pained his heart. "Is this what you've been reduced to again? Drowning your sorrows in cheap whiskey? At least buy the good stuff."

John's head snapped up, eyes widening as Odelia's spectral form materialised beside him, her pale dress billowing in an ethereal breeze. "Odelia?" he croaked, his voice rough from disuse and grief. "What are you...how...?"

"Darling, you should know by now that I never could stay away from you," Odelia quipped, her ghostly lips curving into a wry smile. "Even death couldn't keep me from watching over my dear, brooding husband."

John's fingers tightened around the bottle, his knuckles turning white. "I'm a waste of space, why bother with me," he whispered, his voice trembling. "Clearly I am not going to change."

Odelia's translucent hand reached out, hovering just above John's shoulder, her eyes softening with an unspoken understanding. "You can't keep torturing yourself like this, John. It's eating you alive."

The dimming light cast longer shadows across the room, reaching out as if to strangle him. John's eyes fixated on the photographs scattered across the desk, each betraying a sign she had not been okay. He traced his fingers over the image of his beloved, a tear falling onto her smiling face. The guilt weighed heavy on his chest, suffocating him. How could he ever forgive himself for failing to protect her? How could he move on when her blood still stained his hands?

"I don't deserve peace," he murmured, his voice accompanied by the crackling of the dying fire.

Odelia settled beside him, her voice taking on a gentle, almost pleading tone. "John, my love, you can't let this consume you. She needs you."

John sobbed with his head in his hands, his gaze fixed on the fading embers in the fireplace.

"Who? You're dead. The girl is dead." his voice strained. "I can't go and give Rose Thompson her daughter back can I?"

Odelia's ghostly figure drifted closer, her ethereal presence filling the room with a cold, otherworldly chill. "John, my darling," she murmured, her voice soft and soothing, "you must let go of that burden. It was never yours to bear."

John's palm was slippery with sweat as he raised the familiar bottle to his mouth. The liquid inside, now lukewarm, swirled against the glass, almost mocking him. He paused, looking into Odelia's spectral gaze that seemed to radiate in the low light. Her disapproval cut through him as he took another gulp, yet he also felt the enduring love and compassion that had always existed between them, even in death.

With a shaky breath, he lowered the bottle, setting it aside on the table. "I don't know how to let go."

Odelia's ghostly hand reached out, her fingers brushing against John's cheek, leaving a trail of icy tingles in their wake. "Go help her, John."

John closed his eyes, savouring the memory of her gentle caress against his skin. His heart ached with a longing that could never be fulfilled, like a wound that would never fully heal. As he stood in the depths of his grief, he knew she was right. He couldn't let this consuming pain overtake him, couldn't let the darkness claim his soul and leave him empty and lost. But he knew he had to stay strong, for her and for himself. He took a deep breath, letting the cool night air fill his lungs and push out the pain and despair.

With a heavy sigh, he opened his eyes, meeting Odelia's gaze once more. "Vivienne?" he asked, already knowing who she meant. "She's okay, she just needs space I think."

Odelia shimmered in the dim light, her eyes filled with a profound understanding that transcended the veil between life and death. "John, my darling," she began, her aristocratic voice softened by the tenderness of her words, "you must go to her."

Odelia's ghostly hand reached out, her fingers hovering just above John's heart. "You did not fail anyone, my love. Nor will you. Go to her, it's important."

She paused, her voice growing stronger, infused with a fierce determination. "You showed me that life was worth living. And now, my darling, it is my turn to remind you of the same. You deserve to be in the land of the living."

"Do you remember when we went to the Alnwick Garden and sat on the swings in the cherry trees? I don't want to give up those memories just yet and I feel like she needs someone present - I just make her feel uncomfortable the entire time."

"John Bassinger! Don't make me start doing poltergeist shit! This moping is tedious and is not going to resurrect me. You cannot save me from this place, and if you cannot, do not imagine that anybody else can."

Her words hung in the air, a lifeline amidst the sea of despair that threatened to drown him. John's eyes met Odelia's, and in that moment, he saw the unwavering faith she had in him, the love that transcended the veil between the living and the dead.

"Orpheus to your Eurydice," he smiled lovingly.

"The cottage," Odelia whispered, her voice carried on the ethereal breeze that rustled through the room. "Please"

John's brow furrowed, his mind grappling with the implications of her words. The thought of returning there, of facing the memories that haunted its halls, sent a shiver down his spine.

Odelia's ghostly hand reached out, hovering just above his own, a whisper of a touch that he could almost feel. "You can, my love. You must. It is the only way forward."

"I'll do it," he whispered, his voice trembling with fear and determination. "For you... I'll return to the cottage and face whatever awaits me there."

"You're not just any detective, John," Odelia teased, her voice filled with a playful lilt that he hadn't heard in far too long. "You're my John, the man who solved the impossible cases, the one who never backed down from a challenge."

A faint smile tugged at the corners of John's lips, his melancholy momentarily lifted by her words. "I'm not sure I'm that man anymore, Odelia. So much has changed..."

Odelia's form circled him. "Nonsense, darling. You're still the same brilliant, stubborn, infuriatingly handsome man I fell in love with all those years ago. And if anyone can unravel the mystery, it's you."

As John stewed upon those words, Odelia began to fade, her features blurring into the shadows of the dimly lit room. He reached out instinctively, desperate to hold onto her for just a moment longer, but his fingers passed through her ethereal figure, leaving him grasping at nothing but air.

She had vanished completely, leaving John alone once more in the emptiness of the living room. But even in her absence, he could still feel her lingering presence like a cool breeze, brushing against his skin and whispering secrets in his ear. It was both comforting and unnerving.

With a trembling movement, he let the full weight of his promise sink into his chest, causing his breath to hitch and his heart to race. He moved towards the window, the moon casting a pale light on his features as he gazed out into the dark night. His mind was a jumbled mess of thoughts and memories, all swirling and colliding in a chaotic dance. The whispered voices and flickering shadows of his past seemed to haunt him even now, but this time, he refused to let them control him.

With determination burning in his eyes, he took a deep breath and clenched his hands into tight fists, feeling the calluses on his palms from years of hard work. He knew that returning to the cottage would mean facing all of his fears and inner demons head-on, but he also knew it was something he had to do. No more running, no more numbing the pain with whiskey bottles and self-pity.

John took a deep, steadying breath, his rich baritone voice filled with a quiet determination as he whispered, "I won't let you down."

The words sat in the air, a solemn vow that seemed to echo through the very fabric of the house itself.

With each step, John's polished dress shoes echoed through the once lively and now silent house. He could feel his posture straightening, a reflex ingrained in him from years of training. But as he reached the door, an ache in his back reminded him that even strong men like him were not immune to the tolls of time.

John reached for his worn leather coat from the pile by the door, its familiarity soothing his unease. Its soft folds provided comfort and protection, shielding him from the cold world outside. He patted the pockets, ensuring his keys and wallet were in place before grasping the handle with a steady hand.

As he emerged into the night, the crisp autumn air hit him like a slap in the face. The icy tendrils snaked beneath his collar and raised goosebumps on his skin, but John barely noticed. His mind was already racing ahead, anticipating the challenges waiting for him.

The pale moonlight cast an eerie glow over the deserted street, creating deep shadows that seemed to move and shift with each passing moment. John's trained eyes scanned the darkness, searching for any sign of movement or threat.

But there was nothing, only the whisper of the wind through the trees and the distant howl of a lonely dog. John released the breath he had been holding, his fingers instinctively tracing the intricate patterns etched into the cool, silver locket that hung around his neck. It contained the tiniest portrait of Odelia, her dark eyes and warm smile captured forever in the delicate metal.

With a lingering look back at the house that had once been his sanctuary, John strode towards his car, his keys jingling in his hand, echoing through the quiet night. He settled into the driver's seat, sinking into the worn leather as he turned the key in the ignition.

The engine roared to life with a deep growl, reverberating through the stillness like the bellow of some ancient beast. John gripped the steering wheel tightly, his knuckles turning white as he put the car in gear and pulled out onto the empty road.

As he drove, the street lights flickered by in a disjointed rhythm, casting harsh beams of light over his face. The lines etched into his features spoke of both grief and determination as he pressed forward on the moonlit asphalt, unsure of where exactly it would lead him. But one thing was certain - John was ready to confront whatever lay ahead, to finally face and conquer the demons that had haunted him for so long.

CHAPTER 12

Wait

Narrator's Note 8.26.3.13 - Life spares not even a solitary individual.

"Vivienne?" John's voice echoed through the empty house, but there was no reply. However, a deep chuckle, seemingly coming from nowhere, sent shivers down his spine and caused his muscles to tense. He quickly kicked off his shoes, feeling the cold of the wooden floor against his bare feet, and shed his coat with a sense of urgency.

As he made his way through the dark corridors of the old house, John's heart thrummed in his chest. The only sound was the faint thud of skin on wood beneath his steps. He searched each room for any sign of life but found nothing but dust and scattered belongings. It was as if the house itself had been abandoned for years.

But just as he was about to give up hope, John spotted a letter propped up on the kitchen table, its edges slightly raised as if it had been placed there with care. His name was written in familiar script on the front, sending a chill dancing across his arms.

He opened it.

The yellowed paper trembled in John's calloused hands, Vivienne's elegant script blurred by the tears welling in his eyes. Her words, etched in black ink, screamed out from the page—a final cry of anguish from a tortured soul.

"I hope that someday, you'll be able to forgive me for this," she had written, the words ill-formed. "I know that my actions will cause you immeasurable pain, but please know that I am doing this to free myself from this pit. The sea will take me and I will be gone, there will be nothing else to do."

John's heart constricted, a physical pain blossoming in his chest. The note slipped from his fingers, fluttering to the floor like a fateful autumn leaf heralding the arrival of winter. "Oh Vivienne," he choked out, her name a broken plea on his lips. "What have you done?"

Desperation seized him, propelling him into action. He couldn't lose her, not like this, not when the wounds of his own loss were still so raw and bleeding. Images of his beloved wife, cold and still in her coffin, flooded his mind. The thought of Vivienne suffering the same fate was unbearable.

"No...no," His voice shook with panic as he snatched up his coat, not bothering with the buttons or his shoes as he rushed out the door. The wind whipped at his face, cold and biting, but he barely felt it. All that mattered was reaching her in time before the sea swallowed her forever.

His feet pounded against the earth as he ran, a man possessed by a single, driving purpose. It pulsed through his veins, drowning out the burn in his lungs and the ache in his legs. He had failed his wife, unable to protect her from the illness that ravaged her. He would not fail Vivienne too. Not this time. Not if there was any chance, any hope of pulling her back from the precipice of despair.

The sound of waves crashing against the shore grew louder, spurring him onward. In the distance, he could see the angry grey sea churning and frothing. And there, a lone figure, floating in the surf...

"VIVIENNE!" he roared, his cry swallowed by the howling wind. "Don't do this! Please!"

The path to the secluded beach was treacherous, a winding trail of sharp rocks and uneven terrain that threatened to send him sprawling with every step. John's feet, clad only in skin, had no protection against the jagged edges that tore at his soles. Pain lanced through his feet with each stride, hot blood seeping into the ground, but he pushed on, undeterred. The physical pain was nothing compared to the anguish that gripped his heart, the fear of losing Vivienne consuming his every thought.

His mind raced, replaying the haunting words from her suicide note, each line a dagger to his already wounded soul. How had he not seen the depths of her despair? How had he been so blind to her silent suffering? How was this happening again? The guilt weighed heavy on his shoulders, a burden he would carry for the rest of his days if he failed to reach her in time.

The salty air stung his eyes and filled his lungs as he neared the beach, the roar of the waves deafening. His gaze frantically searched the shoreline, seeking any sign of Vivienne amidst the chaos of the churning sea. Time seemed to slow, each second an eternity as he scanned the horizon, his heart pounding in his ears.

And then he saw her, a fragile silhouette against the raging tide, her arms outstretched as if welcoming the embrace of the merciless waves. "Vivienne!" he cried out, his voice raw with desperation. "I'm coming! Hold on, please!"

John's voice was drowned out by the crashing waves, his desperate plea carried away by the wind. He ran faster, his muscles burning with exertion as he closed the distance between them. The sand beneath his feet shifted and gave way, making each step a battle against the elements.

As he drew nearer, he could see Vivienne's face, her once vibrant features now etched with sorrow and despair. Her eyes, once sparkling with life, were now hollow and vacant, staring out into the vast expanse of the sea. The sight of her so broken and lost tore at John's heart.

"Vivienne," he called out again, his voice hoarse and strained. "I'm here. I'm here for you. Please, don't do this."

He reached the water's edge, the icy waves lapping at his ankles, but he paid no heed to the cold. The saltwater crept into his cuts, his feet stinging as if screaming, but he paid no heed to that either. His focus was solely on Vivienne, on reaching her before the sea could claim her forever. He waded deeper into the water, the current tugging at his legs, threatening to pull him under.

"John?" Vivienne's voice was barely audible above the roar of the waves, but he heard it, a flicker of recognition in her haunted eyes. "Why are you here?"

"I'm here because I care about you," John replied, his voice cracking with emotion. "I'm here because I can't lose you, not like this. We can't lose you."

He reached out his hand, his fingers stretching towards her, a lifeline in the storm. "Take my hand, Vivienne. Let me help you. Let me be there for you, as I should have been all along."

Vivienne's gaze locked with John's, a flicker of hesitation in her eyes as she watched his outstretched hand. Everything seemed to drag her deeper into the unforgiving sea, the current swirling around her, threatening to consume her entirely.

John's heart pounded against his chest, his breath coming in short, desperate gasps as he fought against the relentless waves. The saltwater stung his eyes, blurring his vision, but he refused to let Vivienne slip away. He had lost too much already; he couldn't bear to lose her, too.

"Vivienne, please," he pleaded, his voice raw. "I know the pain you're feeling, the darkness that threatens to engulf you. But you're not alone. I'm here, and I will never leave you to face this on your own."

With a rush of determination, John lunged forward, his fingers grasping Vivienne's trembling hand. Her skin was cold and clammy, a stark contrast to the warmth of his own. He tightened his grip, refusing to let go, refusing to let the sea claim another life.

"I've got you," his voice barely discernible above the crashing waves. "I won't let you go, Vivienne. I promise."

As he spoke those words, a flicker of hope ignited in Vivienne's eyes, a faint glimmer of light amidst the darkness that had consumed her. She clung to John's hand, her fingers intertwining with his, a silent plea for salvation.

John's muscles strained as he pulled Vivienne closer, fighting against the current that sought to drag them both under. The waves crashed around them, the salty spray stinging their faces, but he refused to yield. He had come too far, fought too hard, to let the sea claim another victim.

With each laboured breath, John inched closer to the shore, his legs burning with exertion as he pushed through the waist-deep water. Vivienne's weight seemed to increase with every step, her body weakened by the emotional turmoil that had driven her to this desperate act.

"Stay with me, Vivienne," John urged, his voice strained with the effort of their struggle. "Focus on my voice. We're almost there."

Vivienne's eyes locked with his, a flicker of determination sparking to life within their depths. She nodded, her lips pressed together in a thin line as she summoned the last of her strength to aid in their fight against the unrelenting sea.

John's heart threatened to burst from its fleshy cage, in a relentless rhythm that echoed the crashing waves around them. He could feel the burn of his muscles, the ache in his bones, but he refused to give in to the exhaustion that threatened to overtake him.

As they neared the shore, the water's depth began to recede, the ground beneath their feet growing more solid with each step. John's grip on Vivienne's hand never faltered, clinging to one another desperately.

"Just a few more steps, Vivienne," John encouraged. "We're going to make it. Together."

With a final, herculean effort, John surged forward, his feet finding purchase on the sandy shore. He pulled Vivienne along with him, stumbling onto the beach in a tangle of limbs and heavy, gasping breaths. The sea's roar faded behind them, replaced by the sound of their floundering breathing and the distant cry of gulls overhead.

John collapsed onto the sand, his chest heaving as he struggled to catch his breath. Beside him, Vivienne lay still, her eyes closed, her face pale and drawn. Fear gripped John's heart as he reached out to her, his hands trembling as he brushed the wet strands of hair from her face.

"Vivienne?" he whispered, his voice hoarse with emotion. "Can you hear me?"

A moment passed, an eternity in the space of a heartbeat, before Vivienne's eyes fluttered open. She blinked up at him, confusion and exhaustion warring in her gaze. "John?" she murmured, her voice crackling with salt.

Relief flooded through John like a physical force, so powerful that it brought tears to his eyes. He gathered Vivienne into his arms, cradling her against his chest as if she were the most precious thing in the world. In that moment, she was.

"I've got you," his voice broke in an instant. "You're safe now, Vivienne. I promise."

John's arms tightened around her, his lips pressed to her hair. The distant sound of sirens, bound for other tragedies, made him hold her tighter as if he could protect her from any danger. It appeared he would make any number of unkeepable promises to save her.

But as he felt the steady beat of Vivienne's heart against his own, as he heard the softness of her breath against his skin, John felt an uneasy calm. In this moment of shared grief and understanding, a bond had been forged between them that would not easily be broken.

As the adrenaline of the rescue faded, the reality of the situation crashed over John like a tidal wave. The depth of Vivienne's despair, the anguish that had driven her to such desperate measures, would need to be addressed. He couldn't help but feel a sense of guilt, wondering if he could have done more to prevent this, to ease her suffering.

John's grief, still raw and all-consuming, mingled with his concern for Vivienne. He understood the pain all too well, the way it could hollow out one's soul and leave nothing but an aching void in its wake.

"I'm so sorry, Vivienne," he whispered, his voice breaking. "I should have been there for you. I should have seen the signs."

Vivienne shook her head weakly, her hand shakily resting against John's cheek. "It's not your fault," she murmured. "I didn't want anyone to know. I thought I could handle it on my own."

John's heart clenched at the vulnerability in her words, at the realisation that she had been suffering in silence for so long. He knew all too well the temptation to shut out the world, to retreat into oneself in the face of overwhelming grief. But he also knew the dangers of that path, the way it could lead to a darkness from which there was no escape.

It all lay heavy, a tangible force that seemed to bind them together. John knew that their lives had been forever changed by this experience and that they would never be the same.

"I'm here," John murmured, his voice low and soothing. "I'm not going anywhere."

Vivienne's fingers tightened around him, a silent acknowledgment of his words. Her breathing began to slow, the tension in her body gradually easing as she allowed herself to be comforted by his presence.

As the sun began to set over the ocean, casting a warm, golden glow across the sand, John and Vivienne remained locked in their embrace. The sound of the waves crashing against the shore seemed to echo the tumult of their emotions, the ebb and flow of their grief and their hope.

And in that moment, John knew that he had found something precious, something worth fighting for. He had a reason to go on, a purpose that transcended his own pain and suffering.

CHAPTER 13

A Black Sunset

*Narrator's Note 26.8.1.5 -
Be dutiful, be honest, be
fruitful, but above all else,
be kind.*

John's calloused hands, roughened by the latest adventure, tenderly guided Vivienne onto the worn velvet couch. The mournful creak of the aged springs pierced the quiet room, weighed by their weary bodies and troubled minds. As she sank into the tattered cushions, her bruised skin cried out in protest, John's face scrunching in concern. He held her close, his warm embrace providing a sense of safety and solace amidst the darkness.

"Easy now," John murmured, his deep voice resonating with a melancholic timbre.

Tears started to spill from Vivienne's eyes, glistening like shards of shattered glass in the flickering, low candlelight. Her breath hitched as she met John's steady gaze, a tortured confession spilling from her trembling lips. "I...I can't go on like this, John. Something will have to give. My mind... is weak beyond repair."

John felt her words throttle his own grieving heart. In Vivienne's anguished admission, he saw mirrored the desolate wasteland of his trajectory, ravaged by the untimely demise of his beloved wife. How many nights had he stared into the abyss, yearning for release from the relentless torment of loss?

"It is not weakness, nor does such a parasite pray on the weak. My wife was not weak, but it took her all the same." John understood finally what Odelia had meant. Help her. Vivienne looked at him with questioning eyes, her concern for him cutting through, even if only for a moment.

"Your wife?" She asked, sensing his need for confession.

"Odelia. Met her at university, was always a big personality," John began to sob.

"She was fiercely quick-witted and extraordinarily intelligent... perpetually affectionate and riotously funny with an exquisite talent for anything you could think of. But none of it saved her. The day I found her... in the garden...hanging there," he trailed off, pain etched on his features. Vivienne squeezed his hand with hers, the sensation grounding him, bringing him back into the room.

"I'm sorry, I'm so sorry, I didn't know..." Vivienne could not look him in the eye, nor bear to see the further damage she had inflicted on this poor man, a stranger who had tried to help despite it all.

With a gentleness that belied his imposing stature, John settled next to Vivienne, the aged leather of his jacket whispering against the faded brocade. "Vivienne," he began, his voice a soothing balm, "I understand the allure, truly I do. But you must believe me when I say it is not the answer."

Vivienne's haunted gaze met John's, a flicker of desperate hope struggling to surface. "But how can I go on, John? The pain, it's...it's unbearable. I'm drowning in it, with no end in sight. It's always been here."

John's calloused hand reached out, tentatively covering Vivienne's trembling fingers. The warmth of his touch was a beacon in the chilling depths of her sorrow. "I know, Vivienne. Believe me. I know." His voice, rich and deep, carried the echoes of his grief. "When Odelia...when she took her own life, I thought my world had ended. The days bled into nights, and I couldn't see a future without her in it."

He paused, the memories of those dark days threatening to overwhelm him. Yet he pressed on, knowing his words could guide Vivienne back from the precipice. "But in time, I realised that Odelia's choice was not a reflection of my worth, nor of the love we shared. Her death was a tragedy, but it need not define the rest of my life. And the same is true for you, Vivienne."

As John spoke, Vivienne felt the icy grip of despair begin to loosen its hold. His words, born of shared pain and hard-won wisdom, seeped into the cracks of her fractured heart, offering a glimmer of solace amidst the darkness. Perhaps, just perhaps, there was another way forward, a path that did not lead to the eternal abyss.

Vivienne's tear-streaked face softened, her eyes searching John's for a glimmer of solace. In the emerald depths of his gaze, she found not pity, but understanding—a profound empathy that could only be born of shared suffering. The weight of her despair, so long her constant companion, began to shift, making room for the faintest flicker of hope.

"How?" she whispered, her voice hoarse from the tears she had shed. "How do you go on, knowing that the one you loved most in this world chose to leave you behind?" The question sat between them, a plea for guidance from a soul lost in the labyrinth of grief.

John's hand tightened around hers, a lifeline in the storm of emotions. "You take it one day at a time, Vivienne. You allow yourself to feel the pain, the anger, the confusion. You lean on those who care for you, even when you feel like pushing them away." His voice gentle, his words a salve for her wounded spirit.

At that moment, Vivienne realised that John's presence in her life was no mere coincidence. He had been sent to her - she knew not by whom but was grateful for it nonetheless.

As if reading her thoughts, John smiled softly, his eyes shining with a newfound tenderness.

John's hands trembled slightly as he reached down to gingerly cradle his bare feet, now reduced to a mess of bloodied flesh and torn skin. The excruciating stinging sensation was becoming unbearable, shooting through his entire body in agonising jolts. His once smooth soles were ragged and raw, resembling a battlefield after a fierce battle. Every step felt like walking on shards of glass, each movement sending waves of pain pulsing through him.

Vivienne observed him with a deep sense of gratitude and a growing connection. Her heart swelled with warmth as she rose from the couch, her movements careful and deliberate. She limped gracefully to the kitchen, her footsteps echoing in the quiet room. The tinkling sound of running water filled the space as she turned on the tap, filling a basin with warm water. Steam rose from the surface, swirling in delicate wisps that seemed to dance in the air. With deft fingers, she added a few drops of witch hazel to the water, its soothing scent immediately enveloping the cottage.

As she carried the basin back to the living room, John looked up at her, his eyes filled with curiosity and vulnerability. "What are you doing?" he asked softly, his voice gravelly.

Vivienne smiled, a gentle curve of her lips that held a promise of comfort. "Let me take care of you, John. Just as you've been taking care of me."

Vivienne knelt reverently before him, resting the basin on the floor next to her, and gently lifted one of his feet, lowering it into the warm water. John inhaled sharply, the sensation both foreign and welcome, as the heat seeped into his tired muscles, easing the ache that had settled deep within. With gentle yet firm strokes, she massaged the arch of his foot, washing clean the blood and dirt that covered them, tracing the contours of his skin with her fingers. John closed his eyes and let out a contented moan, feeling not just physical relief but also emotional weight lifted off his shoulders as he surrendered to her care and attention.

Within that moment, the rest of the world fell away, leaving only the two of them, conversing in unspoken words, the silence comfortable. The cottage seemed to hold its breath, its husk bearing witness to the tender exchange, and for once did not seek to intervene.

As Vivienne's fingers worked their magic, John felt his tension dissipate, as though it were being washed away too. He looked down at her kneeling at the foot of the sofa, leaning slightly on its frame.

"I haven't been cared for like this in a long time," John croaked, his voice succumbing to the day's stresses. "Not since..." He trailed off, the memory of Odelia's tender touch a bittersweet ache in his heart.

Vivienne looked up at him, her eyes shimmering with understanding. "It's okay to feel, John. To grieve, to hurt, to heal. You've been so strong for so long, carrying the weight of the world on your shoulders. A weight I have only added to. Let me help you, just as you've helped me."

John nodded, a single tear escaping the corner of his eye and trailing down his cheek.

Vivienne's gentle care enveloped John like a warm blanket, the warmth of the water and tenderness of her touch creating a sense of addictive comfort. As she tended to his injuries, John finally allowed himself to take a deep breath and relax. Vivienne's hands, steady and purposeful, moved with practiced grace as she retrieved the first aid kit. With meticulous movements, she opened the box and gathered the necessary supplies. John watched, transfixed, as she carefully patted his feet dry with the soft towel, her touch a whisper against his skin.

"This might sting a bit," Vivienne warned, her voice gentle as she uncapped a bottle of antiseptic. John inhaled sharply as the cool liquid made contact with the cuts and scrapes on his feet, the sensation a sharp contrast to the soothing warmth of the water.

Pain is a reminder that we are alive, that we can still feel, even when our hearts are heavy with grief. John understood that all too well.

Vivienne worked in silence, her brow furrowed in concentration as she cleaned each wound with meticulous care. John's eyes never left her face, studying the play of emotions that danced across her delicate features – the sadness that lingered in the corners of her mouth, the determination that shone in her eyes, and the tender affection that softened her gaze.

As she reached for the bandages, Vivienne's fingers brushed against John's ankle, the contact sending a shiver up his spine. In that fleeting moment, he felt a spark of something he thought had been lost forever – a connection as comforting as it was discomforting.

Vivienne wrapped the bandages around John's battered feet, her touch quiet in its vigilance. In the silence of the cottage, broken only by the soft rustling of fabric and their breaths, John felt a little more human.

As she tied off the last bandage, Vivienne looked up at John, her eyes searching his. "There," she whispered, "all done."

John's voice escaped his lips in a hoarse whisper. "Thank you, Vivienne. For everything."

Vivienne's hands lingered on John's feet, almost a little too long, the contact seemingly beginning to be overwhelming.

"John," she began, trembling slightly, "I don't know how to thank you for all you've done. Not just for helping me with the cottage, but for... for being here, for understanding."

John's heart clenched at the raw vulnerability in her words.

"You don't have to thank me," he replied, his voice low and sincere. "We're in this together, Vivienne. We've both been through hell, but maybe... maybe we can find a way out."

As the words left his lips, John realised the truth in them. In helping Vivienne confront her problems, he was confronting his own. The pain of losing Odelia still throbbed like a fresh wound, but he could see the wood for the trees.

John's hand slipped from Vivienne's shoulder, his fingers ghosting down her hair before resting on the sofa cushion. The warmth of her skin seeped into the air, the smell of it a tangible thing. They were both still alive, still breathing, despite it all.

"John," she breathed, her head down like an abused thing. "I... I don't know how to thank you. For everything."

John's lips curved into a sad smile, his green eyes meeting hers in the dim light. "You don't have to thank me, Vivienne. You've thanked me a hundred times. You are worthy of respect and care. It should not be something you feel is a burden to those who show it."

The resulting silence was charged, like an uncomfortable truth, but neither of them pulled away. The connection between them seemed to transcend the boundaries of their individual pain, forging a bond that neither of them had expected.

Vivienne's mural sat proudly before them, gleaming amongst the ruin that lay beyond it. They both stared at it for a time, willing it to change before their eyes, but nothing did. It stubbornly stared back at them, standing as a lone guard.

As they sat in the stillness of the cottage, the immense sorrow seemed to lighten, if only for a time. The flickering candle cast its cloak everywhere, on the face that would not forget what they had seen that day. The beast still lurked beyond the sanctuary of their shared space, and the light was only just arriving.

CHAPTER 14

A King, a Joker and a Thief Walk Into a Bar

Narrator's Note 7.79.4.8 - Do not discount second chances, they are usually the making of someone.

A delicate porcelain vase exploded against the wall, its fragments glinting like sharp diamonds as they scattered across the polished hardwood floor. John's reflexes kicked in and he instinctively ducked to avoid a heavy tome hurtling past his ear before slamming into the cottage wall with a resounding thud. The once peaceful atmosphere was now charged with an unseen energy, thick and vengeful, making every hair on John's skin stand on end. It felt as if even the air itself crackled with danger and foreboding.

"John, look out!" Vivienne cried, her eyes wide with terror.

As the creature's claws tore through the air, John reached for her hand and yanked her behind the sturdy oak table. Books flew from their shelves, pages fluttering like startled birds as the walls groaned under the pressure of the beast's power. Shadows danced in the flickering candlelight, like children at play. John's mind raced, his detective training desperately trying to work through what was happening. But as he looked into the abyss of pure evil before him, he knew this was beyond rational understanding.

In the blink of an eye, a glint of metal caught John's attention. It was a kitchen knife, its blade gleaming wickedly in the dim light. He couldn't comprehend how it had gotten there, suspended in midair for a breathless moment before hurtling towards him with supernatural speed. Time seemed to slow down as he watched the deadly projectile spin end over end, its goal clear: his head.

With adrenaline coursing through his veins, John made a split-second decision. Grabbing Vivienne's hand, he dove to the side, narrowly avoiding the knife that embedded itself in the wall behind them with a sickening thud, the metal quivering in its place. John's heart was racing like a wild animal trapped in a cage, his senses on high alert as he tried to catch his breath.

"Are you alright?" he asked Vivienne, his voice rough with adrenaline and fear.

She nodded mutely, her face ashen in the gloom. John's gaze lingered on the knife, a hair's breadth from where his head had been a moment before. The cold realisation of his mortality settled over him, the spectre of death never closer, never more real.

With a grim set to his jaw, John pushed himself to his feet, offering Vivienne his hand. "We have to find a way to stop this," he said, his voice a low rumble. "Whatever it takes."

Vivienne accepted his proffered hand, her delicate fingers trembling in his calloused grasp, her eyes tracing the outline of his tensed muscles through his shirt. "You think it's her too, don't you?" she whispered, her voice thin and reedy "The murdered girl."

John's brow furrowed, his mind racing with the implications. "It's the only thing that makes sense," his voice betraying his exasperation. "She's trapped here, reliving her final moments, her rage and despair manifesting in these violent outbursts."

Vivienne shuddered, wrapping her arms around herself to ward off a sudden chill. "But why us? Why now?"

"Perhaps we're meant to be the ones to uncover the truth," John mused, his gaze distant as he pondered, "To bring her the peace that was denied her in life."

A floorboard creaked overhead, the sound like a gunshot in a barrel. Vivienne flinched, pressing closer to John's solid form, the scent of his sweetened sweat filling her nose. "How do we even begin?" she asked, her voice trembling with dread and force.

John's mind churned with the possibilities, the old instincts of his detective days stirring to life. "We know the facts," he said, his tone taking on a note of authority. "We've read the newspaper articles, my old police reports, your book from the library, anything that could give us a clearer picture of what happened to her. The one thing we know very little about is the house itself, its history, etc. Its former owner was unhelpful, to say the least..."

Vivienne nodded, her eyes brightening with an idea. "There was a huge amount of detritus in the house but I do recall old boxes in the attic," she said, her voice gaining strength as she latched onto the plan. "Maybe there's something in there that can help us."

John squeezed her hand, a silent promise of protection and support. "Then that's where we'll start," he said, his voice a low rumble.

Together, they made their way towards the attic, the planks creaking beneath their feet like the groans of the damned. The shadows pulsed and writhed around them, the changeling seemingly directing them, its eyes locked on its prey. But John's resolve only hardened, his steps sure and unwavering as he led Vivienne into the heart of the mystery, determined to unravel the twisted skein of the past and bring a small measure of peace to the tortured soul that haunted these walls.

The attic was a cluttered labyrinth of forgotten relics and dust-shrouded memories. Vivienne and John picked their way through the maze of boxes and trunks, each step raising a cloud of musty, stale air that tickled their noses. The scent of age and dirt permeated the space, clinging to every object like a silent reminder of time's passage. Moths had eaten through a multitude of fabric, leaving behind tattered remnants of once precious items. Yet, amidst the ruins lay a trove of forgotten treasures. Vivienne's sharp eyes scanned from one stack of papers to the next, searching for any clue that could shed light on the tragic fate of the murdered girl.

"Look at this," she said, her voice hushed with reverence as she pulled a yellowed newspaper clipping from a battered leather portfolio. "Photos of the house as it was being built, oh and this must be the Sawyer Family from my book."

John leaned in, his eyes scanning the faded print. "The Sawyers lived here for some years but left for the South way before our case, they started a particularly insidious cult," he reeled off, his brow furrowing. "Brainwashed several people into committing some heinous crimes but we could find no link to our case."

Vivienne shuddered, a chill racing down her body. "What on earth is this," she said, her finger tracing the characters in the photo. "That figure's not the fault of the camera is it."

John's jaw tightened, his mind already racing ahead. "No," he said, his voice thrumming with anticipation. "Let's set these aside to bring downstairs."

They spent hours in the attic, pouring over every scrap of information they could find. By the time they emerged, the sun had not long departed, leaving the cottage at the mercy of dusk. But they had a plan now, a purpose that drove them forward.

"Tomorrow, we go through all these properly," John said, his voice low in the gathering dark. "And go to see Tim Shelley, Emily's teacher. I always thought he knew more than he was letting on, he might speak to you."

Vivienne nodded, her eyes glinting.

The next morning, a cold and grey dawn greeted Vivienne and John as they set out to meet Tim. A heavy mist hung low over the village, making it difficult to see ahead. Despite the early hour, both of them were dressed in layers, their breath forming white puffs in the chilly air. The events of the previous days weighed heavily on their minds, and they walked in silence, lost in their thoughts.

Vivienne's eyelids drooped as she struggled to keep her tired eyes open. She had drifted off a few times during the journey, leaning against John for support. But even when awake, she couldn't shake off the unease deep within her. Every shadow seemed menacing, every rustle of leaves a potential threat.

As they passed through the countryside, Vivienne couldn't help but notice how different it all looked now. The once beautiful rolling hills and craggy cliffs now appeared ominous and foreboding. And with each passing mile, her anxiety grew stronger.

Finally, they reached their destination - a small, dilapidated house on the outskirts of town. The windows were boarded up and the exterior walls were peeling paint in jagged strips. Vivienne and John exchanged a knowing look, wordlessly acknowledging one another.

With a deep breath, John reached out and knocked on the door, the sound echoing through the air like a crack of glacial ice. For a long moment, there was nothing but silence. And then, slowly, the door creaked open, revealing a face that Vivienne had only seen in faded photographs and police sketches.

Standing there on the threshold of the unknown, Vivienne felt a familiar bubbling of fear, a primal terror that threatened to overwhelm her. But she pushed it down, focusing instead on the task at hand. The man gestured inwards through gritted teeth, surveying John intently, and Vivienne carefully climbed inside, avoiding contact with any surface.

John followed Vivienne into the dimly lit interior, his keen detective's instincts on high alert. The dank scent of mould assaulted their nostrils as they cautiously navigated the filthy space. The man who had answered the door, a gaunt figure with haunted eyes, regarded them warily.

"What do you want?" he rasped, his voice like sandpaper against their ears.

Vivienne stepped forward, her voice steady despite the hammering of her heart. "We're here about the murder of the young girl, the one from the cottage. We believe you may have information that could help us solve the case."

The man's eyes narrowed, a flicker of something dark and dangerous passing across his features. "I don't know what you're talking about," he growled. "I've got nothing to say to you."

John's hand tightened on Vivienne's arm, a silent warning to tread carefully. "Listen," he said, his deep voice resonating, rippling around the room. "We're not here to cause trouble. We just want the truth. If you know something, anything at all, it could help us put an end to this nightmare."

The man hesitated, his gaze darting between them like a trapped animal. Vivienne could see the internal struggle playing out across his face, the warring desires to protect his secrets and to unburden himself.

"Please," she whispered, her voice barely audible over the pounding of her own heart. "Help us. Help her."

For a long moment, the man remained silent, his eyes searching their faces for any sign of deceit. And then, slowly, he nodded. "Alright," he said, his voice heavy with resignation. "I'll tell you what I know. But you have to promise me two things."

John and Vivienne exchanged a glance, a silent communication passing between them. "What is it?" John asked, his voice carefully neutral.

The man's gaze bore into them, his eyes haunted by the ghosts of his past. "Promise me that you'll find the bastard who did this. Promise me that you'll make him pay for what he's done. And keep me well out of it."

With a solemn nod, she made the promise that changed everything. "We will," she said, her voice ringing with conviction. "We'll find him. And we'll make sure he never hurts anyone ever again. No one need know we were here."

As the man began to speak, his words tumbling out in a rush of long-buried secrets and painful truths, Vivienne and John listened intently, their minds mapping out what they were hearing. They knew they were on the cusp of something momentous, a breakthrough that could finally bring peace to the restless spirit that haunted the cottage.

"...I know I should not have had those cameras at that house, but I can tell you for certain. They both went in and neither of them came out again."

CHAPTER 15

Gentle Fingerprints

*Narrator's Note 16.3.1.1 -
Come and wonder at what
curiosity can do.*

For a day and a night, John and Vivienne had been huddled together in the dimly lit kitchen, surrounded by a chaotic mess of faded photographs scattered across the rickety wooden table. The air was thick with tension and the scent of freshly brewed coffee sat forgotten on the counter.

Vivienne leaned forward, her brow furrowed in intense concentration as she studied every detail of the photos. Her dark hair fell in dishevelled strands around her face, evidence of the long hours they had spent trying to crack the case. Beside her, John sat stoically, his broad shoulders hunched slightly as he stared unblinking at the evidence before them.

The room was still except for the occasional rustle of paper or creak of wood as they shifted through the photos.

Vivienne's slender fingers danced across them, pausing on one image in particular. She tilted her head, brown curls grazing her shoulder. "John, look at this," she murmured, tapping the photograph. "The wall in this shot. It looks...different somehow."

John blinked, dragging himself out of the fog that perpetually clouded his mind these days. He leaned closer, the hint of sandalwood enveloping Vivienne as his arm brushed against hers. "Let me see."

He plucked the photo from the table, holding it to the faint light. His eyes were immediately drawn to the wall in the background. It appeared to jut out from the rest of the images, its edges sharp and defined, as if it had been pushed forward by several inches. Was it a trick of the light or something more sinister? As he pondered this, Vivienne's gaze scanned him carefully, her expression soft with understanding. Was it just an illusion caused by the lighting or something more sinister?

"It could be nothing," she offered gently, her lilting voice barely above a whisper. "Just a trick of the camera angle."

John shook his head, jaw clenched tight. "No, you're right. There's something off about it. We need to take a closer look."

He pushed back from the table abruptly, the legs of the chair scraping harshly against the cold, stone floor. Vivienne rose to join him, her emerald green dress cascading down around her like a waterfall of silk. In the flickering candlelight, her alabaster skin seemed to radiate with an angelic glow, captivating his eyes for a slice of time.

Together they turned towards the darkened hallway, each step heavy with trepidation and uncertainty. As they drew closer to the wall in question, the air grew dense and oppressive, filled with the pungent smell of rot that assaulted their senses.

Vivienne reached out a trembling hand, her fingertips ghosting over the rough surface of the wall. "There's something here," she murmured, her brow furrowed in concentration. "A crack, hidden beneath the paint."

John leaned in closer, his breath mingling with hers in the cramped space. Her perfume, a delicate blend of jasmine and rose, filled his nostrils, a smell achingly familiar. With a gentle touch, he traced the outline of the crack, his mind racing with possibilities.

"We need to open it up," he said, his voice rough.

Vivienne nodded, her eyes shining with fierce determination. "I'll get the tools."

Before he could protest, she was bounding away with eager steps. He tilted his head in amusement as he watched her totter on her tiptoes, determined to retrieve his toolbox. Her petite figure strained under the weight as she struggled back towards him, the sound of her footsteps punctuated by occasional grunts and gasps. With a loud thud, she set it down in front of him, beads of sweat forming on her forehead from the effort.

Seeing the concern and bewilderment in his eyes, she started to giggle.

"I'm not completely useless, you know..." she teased, playing with a hammer.

He exhaled a shaky breath and extended his hand, fingers trembling as they grazed the rough edges of the hairline fracture. A surge of adrenaline coursed through his body as he realised the significance of this discovery, the anticipation palpable.

"I never thought I'd find myself here," he murmured, his voice barely above a whisper. "Chasing ghosts, I'm not sure you're the best influence."

Vivienne laughed and placed a gentle hand on his arm, her touch welcome amidst the stewing of his thoughts. "You're not alone, John. We're in this together, remember?"

He nodded, a faint smile tugging at the corners of his lips. "I know. And I'm grateful for that, more than you could ever know."

With grit and determination, they attacked the crack in the wall, their tools scraping against rough surfaces and causing flakes of paint and plaster to fall. Sweat dripped down their faces as they worked, the plaster crumbling beneath their efforts, revealing a small opening that seemed to lead into darkness.

John's heart raced with anticipation as he peered into the void beyond and couldn't shake the feeling that something ominous was lurking on the other side. With one final tug, the last of the plaster gave way, framing the nothingness they had revealed.

As they scanned the space, their flashlights illuminated rickety old walls and dirt floors, not betraying for one moment what might be in store.

As the passageway stretched out before them, a yawning chasm of darkness and despair, Vivienne and John shared a long, meaningful glance, their eyes saying what words could not. They stood at the precipice of the unknown, uncertain of what lay ahead.

With a deep breath to steady his nerves, John crouched down and took the first step into the void. His footfall echoed off the walls, amplifying the eerie stillness that surrounded them. Vivienne followed closely behind, her hand tightly gripping his in the darkness, an anchor against the rising tide of fear that threatened to engulf them both.

As they descended deeper into the passageway, the air grew musty and stale, the weight of the stone walls pressing in on them like an elephant on their chest. Every step felt heavier than the last as they plunged deeper into the depths below.

"John," Vivienne whispered, her voice barely audible above the pounding of their hearts. "Do you feel it? There's something here."

John nodded, his throat constricted with fear and dread, rendering him unable to speak. The hands on their legs were cold and clammy, the texture scaly like a serpent's skin, each stroke leaving behind a slimy residue that made John want to squirm away. But the grip was too strong, forcing him to kick out in a desperate attempt to break free. Vivienne's hand trembled violently in his as he looked back at her, her eyes squeezed shut in a silent prayer for salvation. John knew her aversion to touch and could see the horror etched on her face as she fought against her ingrained response. They pressed on, inch by agonising inch towards the faint sliver of light at the end of the passageway.

They continued cautiously, almost creeping towards the faint light at the end of the passageway. But as they reached the bottom, darkness engulfed them completely. All John could feel was Vivienne's hand in his own, their only anchor in the suffocating darkness. With his other hand, he groped for a door handle until his fingers finally found purchase.

As he pushed open the door, a putrid stench assaulted their senses and Vivienne's steps faltered, her breath catching in her throat as she beheld the gruesome scene before them. A nightmare.

The bunker room stretched out like a twisted canvas of a madman's lair, sending shivers down their spines and causing their stomachs to churn with revulsion at the unspeakable horror.

"Oh my God," she whispered, her voice trembling. "John, look at this."

The walls were adorned with a gruesome display of disturbing photos, each one capturing the lifeless gaze of the deceased. The room was splattered with blood, as if a violent storm had passed through and left its crimson mark on every surface. Trophies taken by the killer lay scattered across dusty shelves - a lock of hair, a bloodstained ribbon, a shattered pair of glasses.

And there, in the centre of the room, a pink silk scarf, stained with blood, was strewn across the floor. Vivienne's bottom lip began to tremble. Emily.

John's jaw clenched and his eyes hardened as he scanned the scene. As a seasoned detective, he had seen his fair share of horrors, but nothing could have prepared him for the palpable sense of evil that lingered in this room. It was as if the very essence of the killer remained, tainting the air with his madness.

What drove him to such depths of depravity? What twisted paths had led him to this bunker, to this altar of his own making?

Beside her, John's breath came in short, sharp gasps. His knuckles turned white as they dug into his palms, veins bulging with the effort to control his emotions. She could feel his rage radiating from him, a seething heat that threatened to spill over at any moment. But there was also an underlying sadness, a deep ache that mirrored her own grief over the tragic events that had taken place within these walls. They shared a silent understanding, their bodies close enough for comfort yet not touching.

"We can't let this happen again," John said, his voice low and intense. "We have to find a way to stop him, to make sure no one else suffers like this."

Vivienne nodded, her resolve hardening even as her heart ached and her hair stood on end.

As they ventured further into the dank, oppressive depths of the bunker, Vivienne and John stumbled upon an unexpected sight. The narrow passageway they had been navigating abruptly ended in a pile of rubble and debris, the remnants of a caved-in tunnel that had once promised escape for the depraved soul who had called this place home.

John's eyes narrowed as he surveyed the scene, his keen detective's instincts whirring to life. "He tried to tunnel his way out," he murmured, his voice echoing off the cold stone walls. "But something went wrong. The tunnel collapsed, trapping him down here."

Vivienne shuddered, her skin crawling. She could almost picture the killer's desperation, his frantic attempts to claw his way to freedom even as the walls closed in around him. It was a fitting end, she thought, for a monster who had brought so much pain and suffering to the world.

With trepidation, they picked their way through the rubble, their hearts pounding in the suffocating silence. And then, as they rounded a final corner, they saw him. A skinless horror, now all but bone, his lifeless eye sockets staring up at the ceiling in a final, eternal accusation.

Vivienne's breath caught, the taste of decomposition sticking to her mouth, her blood running cold at the sight. She had known, intellectually, that they would find him down here. But to see him in the flesh, to confront the reality of his death and the horrors he had wrought, was almost more than she could bear.

"I've been living with this here..." she trailed off.

John's hand found hers in the darkness, his fingers lacing through her own in a silent gesture of comfort and solidarity.

Together, they stood over the body of the man who had haunted their dreams and stolen their peace, the life of a precious daughter.

They had uncovered the dark secrets hidden within this haunted cottage, which had brought the killer's reign of terror to an end. But even as relief washed over them, Vivienne knew the scars left behind would never truly fade. The past had a way of lingering, casting its shadow over the present and the future alike.

And as they stood in the flickering light of the bunker, surrounded by the sickening artefacts of a twisted mind, Vivienne couldn't help but wonder if they would ever truly be free of the weight of it all.

John reached into his pocket with his free hand, his fingers brushing against the cold metal of his phone. He knew what he had to do, knew that it was time to bring this nightmare to an end. But even as he dialled the number for the local authorities, he couldn't help but feel a sense of profound sorrow mingling with relief.

"This is John Bassinger," he said, his voice steady despite all raging within him. "I need to report a crime scene."

As he ended the call, John felt Vivienne's hand tighten around his own, her slender fingers wriggling slightly in his grasp. He turned to look at her, his green eyes searching her face in the dim light. She looked pale and drawn, disgust and alarm etched into the delicate lines around her eyes and mouth.

"It's over," he murmured, his deep voice echoing softly in the confines of the bunker. "We did it, Viv. We found him."

But even as the words left his lips, John knew that it wasn't really over. Not for them. Not after everything they had seen and experienced in this haunted place.

They stood together in silence, their eyes locked on the lifeless body before them, knowing the fear that anchored them here would soon dissipate. The minutes they stretched on, each one feeling like an eternity.

As the distant sound of life restarting on the surface began to pierce the silence, John couldn't shake the feeling that something remained, watching, waiting.

For in the face of such darkness, such unimaginable cruelty, how could anyone ever truly be whole again?

CHAPTER 16

Battlefield

Narrator's Note 10.1.4.2 - It is never too late to try to put things right. Even if you fail, there is reward enough in it.

The harsh hum of fluorescent lights echoed through the police station as John walked through the worn doors, Vivienne trailing behind him. The familiar stench of stale coffee and unwashed bodies greeted them, triggering a wave of uneasy memories for John.

He made his way to the front desk, each step feeling heavier than the last. With trembling hands, he reached into his pocket and pulled out a piece of crumpled paper. The young officer at the desk looked up at John's approach, his eyes widening in recognition as he saw the haunted look on his face.

"We need to speak with Detective Harris. It's about the Emily Thompson case," John said, his deep voice rumbling through the hushed station.

The officer's brow furrowed. "Detective Harris is no longer on that case, sir. It's been over a decade-"

"I'm well aware," John cut him off, jaw clenching. "But we have new evidence. I called but nobody seemed to be interested."

Beside him, Vivienne nodded, her delicate features now hardened. "Please, it's crucial that we speak with whoever is in charge now."

John's pulse quickened as he waited for a response, time slowing to match the unearthly dirge of night working.

The officer hesitated, then reached for the phone. "Let me see what I can do. Wait here."

John's hands trembled as he watched the officer reach for his phone. He turned away, trying to distract himself from the photographs hidden in his coat pocket. The images of shattered innocence, captured in black and white, burned behind his eyelids. His throat constricted as he fought back tears, struggling to keep his composure.

Vivienne's hand found his, her touch grounding amidst the rumbling of his mind. "We're going to make this right, John," she whispered. "For Emily."

John could only nod, not trusting his voice. In the cold, unforgiving light of the police station, he prayed that this time, justice would not be denied.

After what felt like an eternity, the officer returned, his expression inscrutable. "Detective Hanson will see you now," he said, gesturing towards a dimly lit hallway. "Second door on the left."

John and Vivienne shared a tight-lipped look, conveying their unspoken understanding of the gravity of the situation. Their footsteps echoed off the scuffed linoleum as they followed the officer's instructions.

As they neared the door, John's heart pounded against his chest like a relentless drum, his nerves on edge. He took a deep breath, mentally preparing himself for what was to come.

With a determined nod, John pushed open the door to reveal a barren room with sparse furnishings. Detective Hanson sat in the center, his grizzled face shrouded in darkness, his piercing gaze fixed on John with an air of suspicion. Undeterred, John met the detective's stare head-on, eyes blazing with determination. Stepping forward, he placed the folder firmly on the table between them, ready to face whatever challenges lay ahead.

"Detective Hanson," John began, his voice steady despite the turmoil. "We have reason to believe that these photographs, along with the murder weapon and trophies, are connected to the unsolved case from five years ago."

Vivienne took a deep breath and slid the now empty folder across the table to Detective Hanson. She arranged the gruesome evidence in front of him - the photographs were gruesome, capturing the horror and fear in the victims' eyes before their lives were brutally taken. A rusted blade, coated in dried blood, sat with the photos, almost daring the detective to touch it. And scattered among the evidence were twisted trophies, souvenirs from the killer's sickening acts.

John anxiously observed as the detective leaned closer, his sharp eyes scanning each piece of evidence.

Would he understand the connections between these seemingly random objects? Could this be the key to finally getting justice for the families of the victims?

The room was tense as John's thoughts drifted to his wife. Maybe now she could rest. The thing that took him away from her was done, the thing that took her away from him was irreversible. His fists clenched so tightly that his nails broke through his skin, a physical manifestation of his inner turmoil. He fought to maintain control over the emotions threatening to overtake him.

Detective Hanson leaned back in his chair, his eyes narrowing as he regarded John and Vivienne with a mix of scepticism and weariness. "You expect me to believe that this... this collection of oddities is somehow relevant to a case that's been cold for half a decade. I would politely suggest that such a whimsical eye for detail is what got you forcibly retired in the first place," His voice dripped with condescension, each word a sharp blow to their carefully constructed argument.

John's jaw tightened, a flicker of anger igniting within him. He had spent countless sleepless nights poring over evidence, searching for connections others had missed. He would not let the detective's dismissive attitude derail their efforts, not when they were so close to the truth.

"Detective, if you would just take a closer look," Vivienne interjected, her voice calm and measured, soothing John's anger. "The markings on the murder weapon match those found on the victim from the cold case. And these trophies, as disturbing as they are, bear a striking resemblance to the personal effects reported missing from the deceased's property."

John nodded, his eyes locked on the detective's face, searching for any sign of recognition, any glimmer of understanding.

"Please just look," Vivienne pushed.

With a deep breath, John met the detective's gaze, his voice low and urgent. "Detective Hanson, I know what it's like to live with the agony of not knowing, to be haunted by the ghosts of the past. I'm asking you, not just as a former colleague, but as a man who has walked in the shoes of those left behind... Please, give us a chance to prove our case."

The detective leaned back in his chair, his fingertips pressed together as he considered John's words. The room fell silent, the only sound the faint ticking of the clock on the wall, and the tap of Vivienne's shoes against the floor. John's heart pounded in his chest, his breath catching in his throat as he waited for the detective's response.

Slowly, almost imperceptibly, the detective's expression began to shift. His brow furrowed, his eyes narrowing as he studied the evidence before him. "There may be something here," he murmured.

John leaned forward, his voice urgent. "It's Reapers Cottage, it's not far and Vivienne now has the place. At least lock it down and assure yourself"

As the detective's gaze met John's, the atmosphere in the room shifted, the tension thickening until it was almost visible. At that moment, John saw the realisation dawning in the detective's eyes, the weight of the evidence finally sinking in.

"My God," the detective breathed, his voice tinged with disbelief and dawning comprehension. "This is actually real, isn't it? To be honest, I had thought you were winding me up."

"Very well," Hanson picked up one of the photos, the horrors playing like a movie in his head.

John nodded, his own emotions threatening to overwhelm him. He thought of Emily, the countless nights he had spent pouring over the case files, searching for the truth that had eluded him for so long. Now, in this tiny, dimly lit room, he could feel the pieces falling into place, the puzzle finally revealing its secrets.

The detective rose from his chair, his movements slow and deliberate. "I'll need to review the evidence, to cross-reference it with our files," he said, his voice steady despite the stakes. "But if what you've brought me checks out... we may finally have a chance to close this case, once and for all."

As the detective's words hung in the air, lingering like a weight on John's joints, a mixture of relief and anticipation flooded through him, but it was overshadowed by the constant ache of loss that had become a part of him.

In the tense silence of the room, every sound seemed amplified - the rustling of papers, the clicking of keys on a keyboard, the soft hum of a fan. The detective's hand reached for the phone with purpose, dialling a number that could potentially change everything. John exchanged a glance with Vivienne, their hearts beating in unison as they awaited confirmation.

Hours passed in restless waiting, as officers combed through the house, searching for clues to unravel the alarming tale that had unfolded within its walls. John and Vivienne provided their fingerprints and DNA, their minds racing with thoughts of Emily and what could have happened to her. The police station buzzed with activity, a symphony of voices and machines working towards one goal. John's mind wandered, images of Emily's lifeless body intertwining with memories of happier times. He could feel Vivienne's presence beside him, a now familiar comfort.

Finally, the door swung open, revealing two uniformed officers with sombre expressions on their faces. They moved with reverence as they entered the room, each step deliberate and precise. In their hands were files containing evidence from the crime scene.

Gloved hands reached out for that which remained on the desk, gently lifting each item and examining it with a critical eye. Photographs were slipped into clear plastic sleeves, the murder weapon was sealed in a sterile bag, and the trophies were carefully labelled and catalogued. Each piece of the puzzle was meticulously packaged - proof of the importance of the task.

As he watched the officers work, John felt a strange sense of detachment wash over him - as if an observer, not a participant.

The final piece of evidence was sealed away, and the officers stepped back, their job complete. The detective rose once more, his hand outstretched in gratitude and respect. "Thank you," he said, his voice thick with emotion. "For your persistence, your dedication. The house has been fully examined, you may return home. We'll take it from here."

John's rough, calloused hand gripped the detective's firm, warm one. They stood in front of the police station, their faces set. Vivienne stood by John's side, her petite frame disguising a dignified strength. Together, they were a force to be reckoned with. As they walked out into the chilly morning air, adrenaline still pumping through their veins, they shared a triumphant smile. No signs of exhaustion showed on their faces - only fierce determination and a deep satisfaction for what they had achieved so far.

A sudden flash of movement caught his eye, and he looked up to see a solitary figure approaching him. As she drew near, her features came into focus - it was a woman, her face etched with deep lines of sorrow, her eyes red and puffy as if she had been crying for hours. His heart froze in recognition as the name came through his mind, his breath hitching in his throat, his feet faltering for mere seconds. Rose Thompson.

She drew closer, her steps softening as she neared him. "Detective Bassinger," she whispered, the title swimming around John's head like an unwanted thought. "I... I heard about what you did. About the evidence you found."

John straightened his back, his towering frame dwarfing her small, hunched form. "I'm so sorry," he said, his deep voice rougher than ever. "I'm sorry I couldn't bring you justice sooner."

The woman shook her head, a sad smile playing at the corners of her mouth. "You never gave up," she said, her words filled with a quiet intensity. "You kept fighting, even when everyone else had moved on. That means more to me than you could ever know."

John felt the weight of her words settle upon him, a burden he had carried for far too long. The guilt of his failure, the knowledge that he had let this woman down, had eaten away at him for years. And now, to hear her gratitude, her appreciation for his efforts, was almost more than he could bear.

"I should have done more," he said, unwilling to accept a thankfulness he felt misplaced. "I should have found the killer sooner. I should have given you closure."

The woman reached out, her hand trembling as she placed it on his arm. "You did everything you could," she said, eyes searching his face. "I know that now. And I know that my daughter can finally rest in peace, knowing that justice will be served."

John felt a lump rising in his throat, and he swallowed hard, trying to keep his emotions in check. But the mother's words had struck a chord deep within him, reminding him of the lives that had been shattered by his failure.

"I'm sorry," he said again, his voice cracking with emotion. "I'm so sorry for everything you've been through."

The mother nodded, a single tear slipping down her cheek. "Thank you," she whispered, her voice filled with a quiet reverence. "Thank you for never giving up on her."

As she turned to leave, John felt a sudden urge to reach out, to offer some words of comfort. But he knew that there was nothing he could say that would ease her pain, nothing that could erase the years of grief and sorrow that had plagued her.

Instead, he watched her go, his heart heavy with the knowledge that he had played a part in her suffering.

He turned away from the retreating figure of the grieving mother, his eyes falling upon the cold, unyielding walls of the police station. His mind churned with the memories of the case, the countless hours he had spent pouring over evidence, searching for the tiniest shred of hope. But in the end, it had all been for naught. He had not seen his wife slipping away, and she had gone.

As he stood there, lost in the depths of his sorrow, a sudden consciousness struck him. He had been given a second chance to make things right.

As he strode from the police station, his footsteps echoing against the pavement, John felt a flicker of hope spark to life within his chest. It was a small thing, fragile and delicate, but it was enough. Enough to keep him moving forward, enough to light the way through the shadows that haunted his every waking moment.

And so, with a heart heavy with sorrow and a soul alight with purpose, Vivienne followed him, ready to face whatever lay ahead.

CHAPTER 17

Tango in the Night

*Narrator's Note 6.36.2.3 -
Houses hold all that has
ever happened within them,
it is a curious power.*

Sunlight poured through the open windows of the quaint cottage, casting dust particles into a mesmerising dance. John's rough, calloused hand reached for the familiar weight of the sander, while Vivienne delicately selected sheets of sandpaper, her graceful fingers fluttering over the varying grits like a skilled pianist selecting keys.

In front of them stood an aged dresser, its once smooth surface now marred by years of use. John's keen eyes traced every line and imperfection, each scratch and gouge telling a story of its own. The paint was chipping away in places, revealing the wood underneath.

"Ready?" Vivienne asked softly.

John nodded, his gaze still fixed on the dresser. "Let's give this old relic a new lease on life."

They set to work, the sander buzzing to life in John's steady grip. The machine roared to life, its vibrations travelling up his arm and resonating deep within his chest. With each pass, the years fell away, revealing the rich, warm hues of the natural wood beneath.

Vivienne stood beside him, her slender frame a graceful contrast to his broadness. She delicately manoeuvred the sander over the intricate carvings, her deft fingers coaxing out every hidden detail with care and precision. John couldn't help but steal glances at her, admiring how she poured her heart into every task, no matter how small. Together, they worked in harmony, their shared passion for woodworking evident in every movement and stroke.

"It's remarkable, isn't it?" she mused, brushing a stray lock of hair from her face. "How something so worn and tired can be made new again, with a little care and attention."

John's throat tightened, her words striking a chord deep within him. "If only it were that easy for people," he smirked, chancing a glance in her direction.

Vivienne paused, her gaze meeting his. In the soft light filtering through the cottage windows, her eyes held an understanding that took his breath away. "Easy's boring," she winked, her voice gentle. "I think you have a distinct disinclination to boredom."

John swallowed hard. When she felt safe enough, Vivienne had a teasing confidence that reminded him sharply of Odelia. It was not fair of him to make that comparison, that much he knew, but grief had him look for her everywhere except her grave. Almost to the point of complete betrayal. He nodded, not trusting himself to speak, and turned back to the task at hand.

They worked in silence for a time, the only sound the steady hum of the sander and the quiet rip of dust billowing in the sunbeams. John lost himself in the rhythm of the work, his mind wandering.

A lump rose in his throat, and he blinked back the tears that threatened to fall. His head ached with confusion, as he looked at the complicated woman beside him. Why had he offered to help?

Hope.

Vivienne's voice cut through his reverie, soft and gentle. "I think these colours will work well in here," she said, holding up a palette of muted greens and blues. "They'll bring a sense of calm and tranquillity, don't you think?"

John nodded, his eyes tracing the delicate swirls of paint. "You have an amazing eye for this," he said, his voice rough with emotion. "I'm not good with such things."

Vivienne smiled, her eyes crinkling at the corners. "It's all about the feeling you want to create," she said, her voice taking on a dreamy quality. "The colours, the textures, the way the light falls across the room. It all works together to create a mood, an atmosphere."

She set the palette down and picked up a brush, dipping it into the paint with a sure hand. John watched, transfixed, as she began to apply the colour to the newly sanded dresser, her strokes confident and precise.

"I think..." Vivienne said softly, her eyes never leaving her work, "This is how I deal with things. I've never really had anyone to talk to and so, I guess I do this instead..."

John felt a tightness in his chest, a yearning he couldn't quite name. He had thought this cottage would be a punishment but it had not turned out so. And he didn't deserve the reprieve.

He moved to her side, his hand hovering over the small of her back. "Where do you want this?" he asked, gesturing to the armchair he had just finished sanding.

Vivienne turned to him, her eyes bright with enthusiasm. "Over by the window, I think," she said, pointing to the far corner of the room. "The light there is perfect, and it will create a cosy little reading nook."

Clumsily, he lifted the chair and carried it across the room, settling it into place with a satisfying thunk. John stepped back, admiring the effect. It was almost unsettling, he thought, how such a small change could transform a space so completely.

He glanced at Vivienne, watching as she continued to paint, her brow furrowed in concentration. She had come into his life like a burst of colour, bright and unexpected and he had no idea what to do next.

"It is important to see the value in everything, I think," Vivienne said, her gaze distant. "Life is a particularly brutal lesson in nurturing the brighter side of humanity. Even in the darkest, most broken things. For what are we, if we are not dreamers."

John nodded, his eyes betraying a deep thought brewing within.

Vivienne set down her paintbrush and reached for a stack of papers on a nearby table. "I've been working on some designs for the remaining murals," she said, spreading the sketches out before them. "I wanted to create something that would reflect the history of this place, but also bring a sense of new life, of hope."

John leaned in closer, studying the intricate lines and swirls of colour. The designs were stunning, a perfection of the old and the new. But there was something else there, too, something that struck a chord deep within him.

"They're perfect," he said, his voice ragged. "They're exactly what this place needs."

Vivienne looked up at him, her eyes shining with gratitude. "Thank you," she said softly. "That means a lot."

For a moment, they stood there, lost in each other's gaze, a tension so palpable it was in danger of overspilling but a tension that neither felt appropriate. But then Vivienne looked away, and the moment passed, slipping away like a half-remembered dream.

"I should get back to work," she said, gathering her sketches. "There's still so much to do."

John shook himself to attention. "Where do you want to start?" he asked, eyes scanning the cottage's walls.

"I think this would be the perfect spot for the centrepiece mural," Vivienne replied, gesturing to the long expanse of plasterboard before them. "It's the first thing people will see when they enter the cottage, and I want it to make a statement."

Side by side, they took turns prepping the wall, their hands working in tandem to fill in every crack and crevice. With each stroke of sandpaper, rough patches were slowly worn down until the surface was smooth and even. John couldn't help but steal glances at Vivienne as they worked side by side. He couldn't help but notice Vivienne's focused expression. Her brow furrowed and her lips pursed as she carefully calculated the measurements.

Within her, a fierce passion burned. It was a fire that refused to be extinguished despite the ever-present darkness surrounding them. He knew this fire well, having once held it within himself, but now it lay dormant, unwilling to be rekindled. The intensity of her flame both drew him in and pushed him away, a reminder of what he had lost and what she still possessed.

As they made progress, the wall took shape beneath their hands, the smooth strokes of the plaster being applied in a steady rhythm. The scent of fresh paint and damp earth filled the air. John let himself get lost in the work, his mind focused solely on the task at hand. In his momentary distraction, he accidentally bumped into Vivienne, causing her to startle and let out a small gasp. His hand lingered too long around her back before he realised his mistake. He could see her mood shift and the panic that his touch had set off. Slowly backing away, he offered a blanket to disguise her trembling as a chill, trying to ease any discomfort or fear caused by his unintentional touch.

"Sorry, John, I, uh... you startled me is all," she stuttered, shaking off the reaction and John's searching eyes.

"I hope I'm not speaking out of turn but, in all this time we have spent in each other's company, why do you still sometimes retreat from an innocent touch, as though it physically pains you? Have I done something to make you afraid?" John asked softly, his deep voice diminishing to a rumble.

His words felt like an accusation, though Vivienne could see in his eyes that it was not. She averted her eyes to the floor, picking at her fingernails. The last thing she had ever wanted to do was hurt anyone, especially him, but her reaction clearly had been hurting him. She let the guilt settle on her, like needles on a pin cushion.

"It is not you, I promise, I'm sorry..." she managed, her voice breaking.

"Don't be sorry, just tell me how to fix it" His superhero complex might be unhealthy but his care did nothing but help. She sighed, smiling defeatedly.

"You know something, John Bassinger? You spoil me. You're like heavily sugared hot chocolate, suffocating the inside of my mouth until I can't taste anything else sweet at all. And you'd have me believing this is what all people are," she said with a teasing indignance.

John's exasperation softened as the realisation hit him - she saw the good in people because she had striven to do so, not because they had shown her.

"So let me spoil you. Let me fix it. Don't deflect. What has you so tied up in knots that being touched is so difficult?" He sat on the armchair and pulled her towards him by her hands, clasping them gently. She didn't take her eyes off their joined hands not even for a second, forcing John to tilt his head to read her face.

She took a deep breath and let it out, calming herself. "It's not all the time. I think it's worse when I'm startled or can't process everything."

"Okay, like now? You won't look away from your hands." John lifted their hands slightly to demonstrate.

"Yes. It feels overwhelming."

"How do I make it not overwhelming?"

"By letting me touch you, rather than you touch me," Vivienne pulled at their hands.

John let go and sat back in the chair, his arms laying along the rests, his hands palm upwards on the ends.

"Is this why you let me carry you out of the water that night..." he trailed off, nervous that alluding to her attempt would finish the conversation, "...because you reached out for me?"

Vivienne nodded, her eyes fidgety.

"My life has been difficult... I have dealt with things I... I associate being touched with violence and if I don't have the time for my brain to untangle the two before you touch me, I'm back there again," she blurted out, backing away from John, her hands clasped behind her back.

John leaned forward on the chair, propping his upper body up with his elbows resting on his knees.

"Okay..." he smiles reassuringly, "...I get it. You need processing time. I feel like a lot more makes sense to me now. That time... those experiences... this is why you spiral?"

Vivienne nodded and swallowed hard. "But I can be okay. I promise. Please do not think you have to worry about me.. or pity me."

"You are not a burden," He raised his eyebrows with an admonishing look.

"I have seen enough as a detective to know that this withdrawal from people is a common response, you haven't told some deep dark secret, even if I am a bit slow on the uptake," he watched her relax her shoulders, "I am a safe space Viv."

She chewed nervously on her lip.

"I haven't always been housed. Not safely. People beat me, set fire to me..." her voice stopped, her throat paralysed in fear. A dawning look slapped across John's face.

"Physical... and sexual violence?" he asked tentatively. Vivienne nodded, unable to look at his face.

"I can't...with detail... not about this... I'm sorry."

John held out his arms beckoning her towards him, and she settled into his lap and allowed herself to be held. They sat there, minutes ticking away, until she raised her head from his chest and reached for the paint palette on the side with a smile. She squeezed his hand, the thank you going unspoken between them but still understood, and pottered back to the wall.

John eventually tore himself away from the mesmerising sight of Vivienne's artistic prowess, his attention drawn to the mundane. The appliances, lifeless and cold, awaited his touch to breathe functionality into their dormant forms. With a heavy sigh, he knelt beside the first of the machines, the cold of his metal tools awakening him from his daydreams.

As his hands worked deftly, connecting wires and tightening screws, John's thoughts raced, his face falling into a stern gaze. Had Odelia seen them, hidden in the shadows, and hurt by his new emotional affair?

Yet, even as he lost himself in the labyrinth of his sorrow, John found solace in the intricacy of his work. The precision required to bring the appliances to life demanded his full concentration, allowing him a momentary reprieve from the relentless grip of his grief.

The hum of the refrigerator, the gentle whoosh of the oven's ignition, these sounds filled the air, mingling with the whisper of Vivienne's brush strokes. The quiet, once comfortable, held an atmosphere of sorts, though if Vivienne felt it, she wasn't giving anything away.

As the hours passed, John and Vivienne found themselves gravitating towards each other again, the warmth of another person a magnetic pull. In the quiet moments between tasks, they sipped tea, examining the fruits of their labours.

For John, these moments of connection were both a balm and a torment, a reminder of all that he had lost and all that he still yearned for. He found himself drawn to Vivienne's gentle strength, her ability to find hope in the darkest of places.

Her mere presence struck a chord deep within John, echoing the very thoughts that had been haunting him since his wife's passing. He felt a sudden, overwhelming urge to confide in her, to share the burden of his grief with someone who might understand.

"I see my wife," he said, his voice barely above a whisper. "She is everywhere... I'm not unconvinced that I'm mad..."

Vivienne set down her brush, turning to face him fully, her eyes filled with sympathy and understanding. "I'm so sorry, John. I can't imagine how difficult that must be."

He nodded, swallowing hard against the lump in his throat.

Vivienne reached out, her hand resting gently on his arm, a simple gesture of comfort and support. "You're not alone, John, and you're certainly not mad. You are grieving, don't fight it."

As he looked into her eyes, John felt a flicker of something he hadn't experienced in months: a sense of connection, of being seen and understood. In that moment, he knew that whatever lay ahead, whatever challenges and obstacles he might face, he wouldn't have to face them alone.

And so, they sat together, two lost souls finding solace in each other's company, the restoration of the cottage momentarily forgotten as they focused on the more important task at hand: the slow, painful process of healing, of finding a way forward in a world that had been forever changed by loss.

But even as he basked in the warmth of Vivienne's presence, John couldn't shake the feeling that something was watching them. His rational mind tried to dismiss it as mere paranoia, a side effect of his overwhelming grief and trauma, but his primal instincts screamed otherwise.

A clenching knot formed in his stomach as he weighed whether or not to alarm her, knowing he had already burdened her enough with his troubles. But before he could even speak a word, the looming danger descended upon them like a crushing vice.

In the deepest, darkest corner of the cottage, a presence stirred, its movements accompanied by the unsettling sound of bones cracking and scales rubbing together. The air itself seemed to shudder as the creature let out a menacing growl.

Without warning, the floorboards beneath their feet began to tremble, a low rumble rising from the depths of the earth. John's heart leaped into his throat as his mind raced, trying to comprehend what was happening.

Then, in the darkness of the adjacent room, two piercing eyes and rows of sharp, jagged teeth emerged from the shadows. Vivienne stood frozen in fear, realising with horror that it was the same face she had seen before - the beast they had mistakenly attributed to poor little Emily Thompson.

They had fixed nothing.

John reached for Vivienne's outstretched hand, his fingers closing around hers in a desperate, protective gesture. "We need to get out of here," he said, his voice low and urgent. "Now."

But even as the words left his lips, John knew it was too late. The cottage had awakened, and the evil that lurked within its walls would not be denied. They were trapped, ensnared in a web of darkness and despair, with no way out but through the very heart of the nightmare that awaited them.

CHAPTER 18

That Thing's Alive

Narrator's Note 4.31.1.3 - Growth is in the little things.

Vivienne stood at the window of her quaint cottage, her delicate fingers clutching the frayed lace curtains as she peered out into the misty landscape. The horizon was shrouded in a thick veil of fog, obscuring any glimpse of the outside world. The sky hung low and heavy, casting a sombre cloak over the village.

But then, like a ghost emerging from the shadows, a dark silhouette emerged from the swirling fog. Vivienne's heart leapt as she recognized John's tall, sturdy form pushing along a strange contraption. As he drew closer, she could make out the outlines of two bicycles, their metal frames glistening dully in the pale morning light. An unexpected excitement coursed through her veins, momentarily erasing the sorrow that had consumed her for so long.

John cut a striking figure in his tattered black leather jacket, his once dark hair now silver-streaked and tousled by the wind. His normally pained expression was replaced with one of determination and purpose as he looked up at Vivienne, framed in the window like a painting. The subtle green of his eyes shone bright, reflecting the glimmer of hope that had returned to their lives.

"Good morning," his deep, resonant voice carried across the wind. "I thought we might try something different today. Have you ever ridden a bicycle before?"

Vivienne opened the door and stepped out to greet him, smoothing her black muslin skirt. "I confess I have not. I'm not sure I have the requisite skills."

A ghost of a smile lifted the corner of John's lips. "No skills needed, just practice. I believe you'll enjoy the freedom it affords. I thought it best for you to have time out of that house for a bit" He laid a large, comforting hand on her shoulder, the most contact propriety would allow. "I shall guide you every step of the way. You need not fear."

He reached out and took her hands in his, sending a surge of warmth through her body, melting away her fears for just a moment. She looked into his eyes, seeing the specks of gold shimmering in his emerald irises that she had not noticed before.

"Very well," Vivienne replied softly, yet teasingly. "I place myself in your capable hands, Detective Bassinger."

John pulled forward the first bicycle, strong forearms flexing beneath his coat sleeves as he set it upright before her. "The key is balance. Let me demonstrate the basics..."

Vivienne stood attentively, her hands clasped tightly in front of her. John's voice was soft and steady as he explained the steps, gesturing animatedly at the bike, with a child-like glint in his eyes. She couldn't believe that just a few days ago, she had been sobbing uncontrollably in this same spot, feeling completely hopeless. But now, as she looked into John's kind eyes and listened to his patient instructions, a spark of hope ignited within her once again.

Though the lesson ahead filled her with trepidation, Vivienne resolved to embrace this new challenge. It got her out of the cottage, which seemed to torment her ever harshly. She had even considered abandoning it, but she had put too much of herself into it to cut the strings that tied her to it. Even in this grey and gothic world, the promise of connection and healing beckoned - if only she dared to reach for it.

With a deep breath, Vivienne mounted the bicycle, her hands gripping the handlebars in a white-knuckled embrace. The contraption wobbled beneath her, an untamed beast threatening to throw her to the ground at any moment. She fought to keep her balance, her body swaying precariously as her feet sought purchase on the pedals.

"I've got you," John reassured her, his deep voice tickling her ears. His large hands hovered mere inches from her waist, ready to catch her should she falter. "Just breathe and focus on finding your centre."

Vivienne nodded, her brow furrowed in concentration as she struggled to master this unfamiliar skill. Each tentative push of the pedals sent the bicycle lurching forward, her heart leaping into her throat with every wobble and sway. Yet, with John's steady presence beside her, she found the courage to persist.

As the minutes ticked by, Vivienne's determination grew, fueled by a desperate need to prove herself capable of something beyond the all-consuming grief that had defined her existence for their entire friendship. She pushed through the fear and frustration, her muscles burning with the effort of keeping the bicycle upright.

"That's it, you're doing great," John encouraged, his words soothing her frayed nerves. "Just a little more, and you'll have it."

And so, with John's gentle reassurance and unwavering support, Vivienne pressed on, determined to conquer this small yet significant challenge. After a few more tries, Vivienne finally found her balance, the bicycle becoming an extension of her body as she pedalled with growing confidence. A wide smile spread across her face, a rare and precious sight that seemed to illuminate the shadows that clung to her like a shroud.

John watched proudly, his heart swelling with joy at her accomplishment. In that moment, he saw a glimpse of the woman Vivienne had once been, before grief had carved its indelible mark upon her soul. The sight of her smile, so fleeting and yet so powerful, stirred something deep within him, a longing to see her happy, to help her rediscover the light that had been so cruelly extinguished.

They rode side by side, Vivienne's full-throated laughter filling the air as she gained speed and freedom, the wind whipping through her hair and caressing her pale skin. It was a sound that John had never heard before, a melody that pierced through the veil of his sorrow and reminded him of the beauty that still existed in this world, even amidst the darkness.

John matched her pace, his laughter mingling with hers, creating a symphony of happiness that seemed to defy the very nature of their gothic surroundings.

As they ventured deeper into the countryside, the gentle babbling of a nearby stream caught Vivienne's attention. She stopped in her tracks, her keen eyes scanning the surrounding landscape for the source of the soothing sound. A sense of wanderlust and excitement coursed through her veins as she turned to John, her eyes sparkling with newfound adventure.

"Shall we take a break? I know a secluded spot just ahead, where we can rest."

John, captivated by the warmth in her voice and the promise of a moment to breathe, nodded his assent. "Lead the way," he said, carrying a hint of anticipation.

As they dismounted their bicycles, the tall grass rustled and swayed around them, kissing their skin with its gentle touch. Hand in hand, they walked toward the hidden oasis, their steps slow and deliberate. A stag, clearly lost, looked curiously at them for a moment, before fleeing. They had thoughts of trying to find it, but Vivienne couldn't bear to look at the fear in its face.

The sound of the stream grew louder with each passing moment, its crystalline waters rushing over smooth rocks and cascading into a pool below. The melodic tones of the stream were a soothing balm to their weary souls, washing away the fatigue and stress of their journey. The air was heavy with the sweet scent of wildflowers and the earthy aroma of rich soil. As they approached the oasis, the cool mist from the water tingled on their skin, refreshing them and invigorating their senses.

At last, they reached the secluded spot, a small clearing nestled beside the crystal-clear waters. Vivienne found a cushioning patch of grass to sit on, free from the damp that plagued the air. They sat, their bicycles resting nearby, and allowed the peace to wash over them.

She turned to him, her voice soft and filled with a vulnerability she rarely allowed herself to show. "Tell me, John, what passion do you wish you had pursued as a child?"

John, surprised by the intimacy of her question, looked at her with questioning eyes.

"I always wanted to do something creative, you know, like learning to sculpt or play the piano, but I didn't have the patience."

"Hmmm..." Vivienne acknowledged and John looked over at her, seeing cogs turning.

As the sun's warmth caressed their faces, Vivienne reached into her bag and retrieved her sketchbook and pencils. With a gentle smile, she turned to John and said, "The beauty of this place is simply breathtaking."

John watched in awe as Vivienne's skilled hands began to glide across the page, her pencil lines transforming the blank canvas into a stunning representation of the landscape before them. The way she captured the play of light and shadow, the intricate details of the foliage, and the serene tranquillity of the stream left him amazed.

As John observed Vivienne, her knitted brows and furrowed concentration drew him in. The paper beneath her hand seemed to sizzle with the energy of her strokes. John found himself drawn to the intensity of her focus, the passion that emanated from her very being. It crackled in the air. Vivienne, sensing John's gaze upon her, looked up from her sketch and met his eyes, their eyes locked in a charged moment of mutual intensity.

Inspired by the moment, Vivienne set aside her sketchbook and turned to John with a mischievous smile. "I have an idea," she said, her voice tinged with excitement. "Why don't we try our hand at sculpting? I have some clay in the cupboards we could use."

John's eyes lit up at the idea, and he nodded eagerly. They quickly packed their bags and hopped on their bikes, pedalling back to the cosy cottage. Vivienne led them to a small cupboard filled with shelves of coloured clay and worktables. Her face beamed as she pulled out some clay and began explaining different techniques they could try.

As they settled into a quiet corner, Vivienne and John's hands eagerly reached for the mound of soft clay in front of them. With skilled movements, they began to shape and mold the formless mass, their fingers dancing across its surface with careful precision. The earthy scent of wet clay lingered in the air, blending with the sweet aroma of fresh flowers on the windowsill.

John's rough, scarred hands trembled as they were guided by Vivienne's delicate fingers, molding the clay into a shape that felt alive. The warmth of her touch seared through his skin, sending electric sparks up his arm and igniting a burning desire he knew he shouldn't indulge in and certainly dared not acknowledge aloud.

As he let go of his inhibitions and allowed himself to explore the medium, he created something raw and personal, a tangible manifestation of the grief and longing that had consumed him for so long.

Vivienne's gaze locked onto John's face, dissecting every crease of determination etched into his forehead, the way his lips pursed in unwavering focus. She released her grip on his hands, acknowledging his progress with a nod before throwing herself into her own project with gusto. Her smile was tinged with competitive fire as she raced against him to complete their tasks.

Their hands were inches apart as they worked together, and each accidental brush made the tension visible once more. The air was thick with unspoken feelings, a forbidden desire that pulsed between them and threatened to break free of their agreed boundaries.

The sun began to set, the light dying enough to make them stop. Vivienne and John stepped back to admire their artwork, their hearts filled with a sense of accomplishment and a shared bond that transcended words. The clay sculptures, raw and imperfect, seemed to fit together. Not like puzzle pieces specifically designed to do so, but nevertheless, one could not imagine one without the other.

Vivienne's gaze drifted to John's face, his chiselled features softened by the fading light. In his eyes, she saw a reflection of her longing, a desperate need for connection in a world that had left them both broken and alone. She felt drawn to him, like a moth to a flame, her body aching to be closer to his.

John's hand reached out, his fingers gently brushing against Vivienne's cheek. To her surprise, she leaned into his touch, her eyes fluttering closed as a sigh escaped her lips. At that moment, all the pain and grief that had haunted them seemed to melt away, replaced by a warmth that spread through their veins like molten gold.

"Vivienne," John whispered, his voice low and husky. "I've never felt this way before. Not since..."

He trailed off, the unspoken name of his late wife hanging heavy in the air between them. Vivienne understood the weight of his words, the depth of his loss. She, too, had known the agony of love ripped away, the hollowness that followed in its wake.

"I know," she murmured, her hand covering his. "But perhaps... perhaps this is a chance for us both. To heal, to find something new."

In the fading light, they found themselves drawn to each other, their bodies moving closer until their lips met in a tender and passionate kiss. Time stood still as they savoured every last second of it.

Vivienne's heart raced as John's arms encircled her, pulling her flush against his broad chest. She could feel the heat of his body through the thin fabric of her dress, the strength of his muscles as they held her close. His lips moved against hers with a fervour that stole her breath away, a desperate hunger mirroring her own.

In that moment, nothing else mattered. Not the ghosts of their pasts, nor the uncertainties of their future. There was only the two of them, lost in each other, their broken pieces fitting together.

As they pulled away, their eyes met, and a silent understanding passed between them. In John's emerald gaze, she understood herself just as well - fractured, scarred, but still alive with the promise of hope. She reached up to caress his stubbled cheek, absorbing the way his skin felt beneath her fingertips, rough and warm and real.

"I never thought I'd feel this way again," John murmured, his voice thick with emotion. "After losing Odelia, I thought my heart had died with her. But you, Vivienne... you've brought me back to life."

Vivienne's eyes glistened with unshed tears, her heart swelling with a love that threatened to consume her. "I was so lost before I met you," she whispered, her voice trembling. "I never believed I deserved happiness, not after everything I've been through. But you've shown me that I'm worthy of love, that I have a future worth fighting for."

As they stood there, lost in each other's embrace, Vivienne's body tensed with immediate dread. A chill ran down her spine as she felt a pair of unseen eyes boring into her. She glanced over John's shoulder, her eyes widening as she caught a glimpse of a ghostly figure in the shadows. It was Odelia, lurking in the shadows, her pale form glimmering under the moonlight, her face a mask of sorrow and longing.

For a moment, Vivienne's heart constricted with guilt and fear. But then she saw the small, sad smile that played at the corners of Odelia's mouth, a silent blessing from beyond the grave.

At that moment, Vivienne realised that she was not just being watched by a vengeful spirit, but witnessed by a benevolent one. And with that understanding came a sense of peace and acceptance, knowing that the power in the cottage was not all bad.

With a sigh, Vivienne closed her eyes and rested her head against John's chest, listening to the steady thrum of his heartbeat.

CHAPTER 19

Paradise on a Friday Night

Narrator's Note 17.5.1.3 - There is no critic harsher than the thinking self.

Vivienne stood rooted to the spot in the backyard of the dilapidated cottage, her emerald eyes transfixed on the grotesque and otherworldly creature writhing and thrashing with an otherworldly vigour within. Its scaly black skin shimmered under the faint rays of moonlight, sending shivers down Vivienne's spine. The once peaceful garden now trembled and quaked as if in fear, disturbed by the presence of this monstrous being. Beside her, John Bassinger remained equally motionless, his face etched with a mirrored expression of terror and apprehension. His hands shook at his sides as he struggled to maintain his composure in the face of such an unearthly sight. Vivienne's heart raced as she braced herself for whatever horrors may come next.

"It's growing stronger," Vivienne whispered, her voice trembling as she watched the creature's frenzied movements through the old, battered window.

John's knuckles turned white as he clenched his jaw in frustration. He reached for Vivienne, and pulled her close, her hands stroking the top of his, seeking comfort and protection. Vivienne felt the roughness of John's work-worn skin against her sides, the still unfamiliar touch now comforting. The barren backyard was overgrown with intertwined weeds and thorns, their weaving stems watching on. They stood frozen, helpless against the poltergeist within.

The entity inside continued to thrash and slam against the walls, its deafening roars sending shivers down their spines. This was an unimaginable nightmare they could not escape from, united by grief and bonded by fear. As they trembled together, Vivienne couldn't help but wonder how they ended up in this horrifying place, where sorrow and terror were the only emotions that reigned supreme.

Vivienne's hands shook uncontrollably as she begrudgingly broke free of John's grasp, her entire body quivering with terror as she reached for the ancient door handle, its rusted metal sending a deathly chill through her fingertips.

Forcing herself to take one last deep breath, Vivienne steeled her resolve and flung the door open, bracing for the horrors that awaited her on the other side. John's presence behind her was a small comfort, a thin shield against the encroaching danger.

But as they stepped over the threshold, the hinges let out an ear-piercing scream, tearing through the silence like a banshee's cry. The sound reverberated through the desolate cottage, setting their nerves on edge and causing Vivienne's heart to race even faster.

With each step into the dark and musty interior, Vivienne felt like she was descending deeper into hell itself. The air reeked of sulphur and decay, and she couldn't shake off the feeling that evil eyes were watching their every move from the shadows. But with John's reassuring hand on her shoulder, they pressed on together.

And then, as suddenly as it had begun, the activity ceased. It was as silent as graves, its abruptness almost more unnerving than the chaos that had preceded it, a palpable sense of menace lurking just beneath the surface. Vivienne and John exchanged a wary glance, their hearts hammering in unison as they wondered what fresh horrors it had in store for them.

"It's gone quiet," John murmured, his voice barely above a whisper. "Too quiet." He scanned the shadows, his detective's instincts on high alert as he searched for any sign of the creature's presence.

Vivienne stood on high alert, her senses straining to pierce the unnerving stillness in the air. She could sense its presence lurking nearby, waiting for an opportunity to strike again.

John took a deep breath and stepped into the bathroom. His eyes scanned the decrepit space with a critical eye, taking note of the cracked and stained tiles, rusted fixtures, and peeling wallpaper. But beneath the decay, he saw potential. He imagined bringing new life to these ruins, transforming them into something beautiful once more.

"We'll start with the plumbing," he said, his voice echoing off the bare walls. "If we can get the water running again, the rest will follow."

Vivienne nodded, her gaze drawn to the shattered mirror above the sink. For a moment, she caught a glimpse of her own reflection, fractured and distorted. But then John was beside her, his strong hands gently guiding her towards the toolbox on the floor.

"We have to continue," he said softly, his eyes holding a promise of something more than just the work.

With a nod, Vivienne reached for a wrench, the weight of it solid and reassuring in her grip. Side by side, they set to work, the steady rhythm of their efforts drowning out the loud silence of the morning's events.

With aching muscles and bruised hands, they toiled to revive the old bathroom. The creature watched their every move from the shadows, biding its time until it could unleash its wrath. And when that moment finally came, it was like a thunderbolt cracking through their bodies, leaving them trembling with fear and disbelief.

John cursed as the pipe he was working on suddenly burst, sending a torrent of water spraying across the room. In an instant, they were both drenched, their clothes clinging to their skin as the icy liquid seeped into their bones.

For a moment, they could only stare at each other in shock, the absurdity of the situation rendering them speechless. But then, slowly, a smile began to tug at the corners of Vivienne's lips, a flicker of mischief dancing in her eyes.

"Well," she said wryly, "I suppose we needed a bath anyway."

And with that, the tension broke, laughter bubbling up deep within them as they surrendered to the moment's chaos. The beast looked on at their resilience with a resentful respect. Not with enough respect that it'd leave them alone though.

With a gentle touch, Vivienne delicately wrapped a soft towel around John's head and began to dry his hair. Her fingers moved precisely, combing through the damp strands as she worked. The warmth of her skin against his own sent shivers down his spine, and he found himself leaning into her touch, sinking into the intimacy between them.

As she finished, Vivienne reached for the sleek hairdryer, its whirring and buzzing filling the room. With each swipe of her arm, she methodically dried his clothes, removing any trace of moisture from them. John couldn't take his eyes off her, captivated by the grace and fluidity of her movements. Even in something as simple as drying his clothes, there was a certain elegance to her that left him at a loss for words.

But as quickly as the moment had begun, it was over, Vivienne stepping back to admire her handiwork with a satisfied nod. "There," she said softly, "good as new."

John's eyes darted to the floor as he muttered a barely audible "thanks." He shuffled his feet, his hands clenched in tight fists. He could feel Vivienne's gaze on him, but he couldn't bring himself to look up. The room felt suffocating, and he wanted nothing more than to escape.

Lost in thought and the job at hand, John barely noticed as Vivienne slipped out of the room, her footsteps echoing down the hallway as she disappeared from view. Over an hour passed by before John realized that Vivienne had left. The emptiness in the room and the silence echoing down the hallway made his heart ache with regret. He realised she was gone, a sudden sense of unease washing over him like a cold wind.

Where could she have gone? he wondered, his mind racing with possibilities. In a place like this, with that thing lurking in every corner, anything could happen.

Driven by a sudden sense of urgency, John set off in search of her, his heart pounding in his chest as he moved from room to room. The cottage seemed to stretch on forever, each shadowy corridor and darkened doorway holding untold dangers that threatened to swallow him whole.

At last, he found her in the kitchen, the warm glow of the oven casting a homey light across the room. The air was filled with the rich, savoury aroma of roasting meat and vegetables, a scent that seemed to chase away the gloom and despair that clung to every corner of the cottage.

"Vivienne?" John called out, his voice rough with concern. "What are you doing in here?"

She turned to face him, her eyes bright with a potent warmth. "I thought we could use a proper meal," she said, gesturing to the oven. "It's been so long since either of us has had anything that wasn't out of a tin or a packet."

John felt a lump rising in his throat as he watched her work, her body moving smoothly and surely as she basted the roast and checked on the potatoes. It was such a simple thing, the act of preparing a meal, but in that moment it seemed to hold a world of meaning.

As he watched her bustling around the kitchen, a plate in one hand and a rag in the other, he couldn't help but feel a twinge of sadness. She was trying to bring some sense of normalcy back into their lives after all that had consumed them. The smell of Sunday roast wafted through the air, mingling with his emotions. But despite her own struggles, she still made an effort to think of others.

"It smells amazing," he said at last, standing beside her at the stove. "Can I help with anything?"

Vivienne smiled up at him, her eyes crinkling at the corners. "You can set the table and help plate up if you like. I've already got the plates and cutlery out of the cupboard."

The wooden cutting board creaked under the weight of the freshly roasted chicken as John slid it onto a platter. He could hear Vivienne humming softly as she arranged the steaming vegetables on a serving dish. The warm, savory scent of herbs and spices filled the air, and for a moment, they both forgot about their troubles.

But as he set the table with mismatched plates and silverware, John couldn't shake the feeling of unease that lingered in the back of his mind. The cottage walls may have provided a temporary shield from the outside world, but he knew that danger still lurked just beyond their reach.

As they sat down to eat, he couldn't help but steal glances at Vivienne, her golden hair catching the light from the flickering candles. For now, they had each other and this small moment of peace. But deep down, he feared it wouldn't be enough when their past finally caught up to them.

John pulled out Vivienne's chair for her as they entered the dining room, the flickering candlelight casting an intimate flush over the carefully laid table. As they settled into their seats, John couldn't help but marvel at the spread before them - the perfectly cooked roast, the crisp vegetables, the fluffy Yorkshire puddings. It was a feast fit for a king, and yet here they were, just two lost souls in a haunted cottage, clinging to this moment.

As they tucked into their food, John caught himself watching Vivienne out of the corner of his eye. The way she savoured each bite, her eyes closing in bliss as she chewed, the small sounds of appreciation she made in the back of her throat - it was almost enough to make him forget the darkness that lurked just beyond the walls.

But even as the thought crossed his mind, the room suddenly grew cold, the candles guttering in an unseen breeze. Vivienne's eyes flew open, her fork clattering to her plate as she looked around in alarm. John was already on his feet, his heart pounding as he scanned the room for any sign of the beast haunting them for days.

And then, without warning, the plates began to rattle on the table, the glasses shaking and clinking together as if possessed by some unseen force. John reached for Vivienne's hand, pulling her close as they watched in horror as the plates suddenly rose into the air, hovering for a moment before smashing to the ground with a sickening crash.

Vivienne let out a small scream, burying her face in John's chest as he wrapped his arms around her protectively. But even as he held her close, John couldn't help but feel a flicker of dark amusement at the absurdity of the situation.

"Well," he said, his voice shaking slightly as he tried to inject some levity into the moment, "at least we don't have to wash them up now."

Vivienne lifted her head, her eyes wide with disbelief as she stared at him. But then, slowly, a small smile began to tug at the corners of her mouth, and before long, they were both laughing - a slightly hysterical, slightly desperate sound that echoed through the empty room.

"And maybe that's all we can do," John murmured, holding Vivienne close as the laughter died away, leaving only the sound of their breathing and the distant howl of the wind outside.

Maybe all they could do was hold on to each other and find what moments of joy they could, even in the face of unimaginable darkness.

With a heavy sigh, Vivienne pulled away from John's embrace, her eyes still bright with unshed tears from fear and laughter. "I suppose I should clean up this mess," she said, gesturing to the shattered remnants of their dinner scattered across the floor.

Without waiting for his response, she swiftly scooped up the broken pieces of glass and made her way to the kitchen sink. The loud clanking of pots and pans filled the living room as she scrubbed away at them, trying to drown out the awkward silence between them.

In a swift and calculated move, John slipped unseen from the room, his eyes scanning for any sign of Vivienne. He reappeared moments later, a massive canvas clutched tightly under one arm and a box overflowing with an array of paints in the other. With delicate steps, he laid out the canvas on the floor, making sure to smooth out any wrinkles or imperfections. His movements were almost reverent as he carefully arranged the paint tubes in front of him, like a painter preparing for their masterpiece.

Vivienne re-emerged at the door, smiling in curiosity at him crouched on the floor.

Vivienne watched as John's hands moved quickly and purposefully, fiddling with the arrangement of it all. Her brow furrowed in confusion, but she didn't want to interrupt his ministrations. Suddenly, he looked up at her with piercing green eyes, his gaze intense and focused. She couldn't help but wonder what he was doing.

"I want you to teach me how to paint," he said, his voice rough. "I want to learn from you, to see the world through your eyes."

Vivienne felt her breath catch in her throat, her heart swelling with a sudden, fierce love for this man who had come into her life so unexpectedly. She knew that he was still grieving, still struggling to come to terms with the loss of his wife. And yet, here he was, reaching out to her, wanting to share in something that meant so much to her.

"Of course," she said softly, kneeling beside him on the floor. "I would be honoured to teach you."

As she began to explain the basics of colour theory and brush technique, she could see him mentally taking notes.

"How do you come up with concepts like that?" he asked, pointing at the mural.

"It's just what's in my head I guess. That one's mainly from flashbacks," she swallowed hard.

"And who is this, in your mind?" he tilted his head and tapped a lone figure toward the edge of the mural.

"Me."

John scooted back to take in the entire mural. At the left edge was a lone figure, features barely discernible, yet was clearly the central character. Blues, yellows, and whites swirled from that edge, depicting a busy city street packed with people, each of their faces unique.

"This is how me, in a spiral, looks - there's a reason it was painted first," Vivienne avoided him with fearful intensity.

Once she had gained the courage, she looked up at John and her heart stuttered in her chest. Silent tears streaked down his face, his eyes distant and haunted. The unsullied brush slipped from his fingers, clattering against the wooden floorboards, a jarring sound that shattered the tranquil moment.

"John?" Vivienne whispered, her voice trembling with concern. She reached out to him, her fingers grazing his arm, feeling the tension thrumming beneath his skin. "What is it? What's wrong?"

"You are exceptionally talented and big-hearted, courageous and unceasingly kind with an emotional intelligence to rival God Himself. That you would think of yourself like this... devastates me."

CHAPTER 20

Just the Socks

Narrator's Note 9.7.3.11 - Some pleasures are universal.

John's face was illuminated by the soft light fluttering in the room as he gazed into Vivienne's captivating eyes. His heart was in turmoil, emotions clashing like a raging storm. Her delicate chin was adorned with cascading brown locks that brushed against his skin as she reached out to touch his hand. Despite the lingering pain of losing Odelia, he couldn't resist the magnetic attraction towards this enchanting woman.

Vivienne reached up, her delicate fingers grazing the silver at his temples, tracing the lines of grief on his face. "Let me help you understand," he whispered, his voice rich.

John's breath caught, his pulse quickening at her touch. The last embers of resistance crumbled to ash as smoldering need consumed him. "I fear I am already lost," he uttered, the words scraping past the lump in his throat.

He claimed her mouth in a searing kiss, pouring his anguish and desperation into her. Vivienne melted against him, fitting into his powerful embrace as if she were made to be there. Yearning to lose himself further, John deepened the kiss, drinking her in like a man possessed.

Their hands fumbled with urgency as they peeled off their paint-stained clothes, tossing them aside without a second thought. In a frenzy, they stumbled backward until they were brought to a halt by the waiting canvas on the floor. Without hesitation, he lowered her onto it, their lips never parting. As they lay entwined, their bodies molded together like pieces of a puzzle. The feel of his skin against hers sent shivers down Vivienne's spine and she couldn't help but let out a soft sigh into his mouth. Their bodies moved in perfect harmony, every curve and plane fitting perfectly, coming together to create one masterpiece.

Guilt pierced him, keen as a dagger's blade. Was he betraying his beloved Odelia's memory by succumbing to carnal temptations in his time of mourning? She was barely cold in her grave, yet here he was, drowning his grief in another woman's arms.

Even as John surrendered to the irresistible pull of Vivienne's delicate touch and alluring perfume, his mind was still plagued with self-doubt and regrets. The familiar arguments and blame that had consumed him for months now seemed to fade into the background as their bodies entwined, seeking solace in each other's embrace. But even as they indulged in this forbidden pleasure, John couldn't help but feel guilty for finding such temporary relief from their shared pain.

Vivienne's hands trembled as she reached for the jars of paint, their bright hues a stark contrast against the canvas's pristine white. With reverent fingers, she unscrewed the lids, revealing the vibrant pigments within. Crimson, sapphire, emerald - each colour seemed to whisper of forbidden delights and untold passions.

John watched, transfixed, as she dipped her delicate fingers into the first jar, the red paint clinging to her skin like the most scandalous of lingerie. His heart raced, pounding against his ribcage as if it yearned to break free from its confines and merge with hers.

"Please," Vivienne breathed, her voice husky with desire.

He could only gasp, words caught in his throat as she dragged her paint-drenched fingers along his chest, etching intricate designs into his feverish skin. The thick, cool texture of the paint coated his skin, sending shivers of pleasure down his spine. The slickness of it made him feel like he was being enveloped in a sensual embrace, its texture foreign to him. The colours swirled and mixed, creating a kaleidoscope of sensations that only heightened his arousal. Each stroke sent a lightning bolt of sensation coursing through his body, igniting every nerve ending with pulsating electricity.

As Vivienne's fingers danced across him, leaving trails of vibrant colour behind, John felt himself falling deeper under her spell. The world around them faded into nothingness, leaving only this exquisite moment pulsing with raw desire and unbridled passion.

With each passing moment, Vivienne's touch grew more bold and commanding. Her strokes became longer and more purposeful, branding him with a secret language only they could understand. John's body trembled beneath her skilled hands, quivering with intense pleasure as waves of heat crashed over him like a raging inferno.

As they pressed their bodies together, John couldn't help feel completed by how perfectly Vivienne fit in his arms. Her curves molded against his, and her skin seemed to seek out every inch of him. As she trailed her fingertips over his abdomen, he caught her hand, a reflexive action to the tender touch. The canvas beneath them was already splattered with vibrant colours, transferring off them to create unusual images. With each brushstroke of her hands, he felt the emptiness dissipate.

"Vivienne," he murmured, his voice ragged. "Are you sure?"

She paused, her eyes locking with his, a tender smile playing on her lips. "As long as you are, John."

John's heart swelled as Vivienne's words echoed in his ears, and he couldn't resist the urge to join her in the colourful chaos. His fingers glided over her back, following the curve of her spine and leaving trails of gold in their wake. He felt a sense of reverence at this moment, holding the precious treasure that was Vivienne in his arms.

As his hands roamed her body, they left behind marks of colour - an inadvertent mosaic. John couldn't help but notice the softness of her skin against his rough, calloused hands. She seemed untouched by the harsh realities of the world, while he bore the scars of a lifetime.

But with Vivienne in his arms and paint coating their bodies, he could forget about his scars and just focus on her. As their passion intensified, their painted hands left behind marks that almost resembled images, a witness to the fire burning between them. And as he gazed at Vivienne's face, her hesitant arousal written all over it, he knew that she too had her own battles and scars - but for now, they were lost in each other's touch.

John's fingers tangled in Vivienne's curly tresses, the silken strands slipping through his grasp like inky rivulets. He breathed in her scent, it piercing through her perfume and drawing him in, and let it wash over him.

"You're everything, Vivienne," he whispered, his lips brushing against the shell of her ear.

As John wrapped his arms around her, Vivienne could feel her heart expanding with warmth and emotion. She couldn't help the tear that rolled down her cheek, leaving a streak of paint in its wake. For so long, she had believed she was unworthy of love or forgiveness, but as she looked into John's eyes, she saw a reflection of her pain and struggles. She felt a glimmer of hope amidst the darkness she had been drowning in.

"And you are, my love," she breathed, her fingers tracing the contours of his face.

Their lips met in a gentle, loving kiss, a subtle confirmation of their unspoken promises for the future. The room dissolved into a blur of colours and sounds, leaving only the sensations of warmth and intimacy between them. Their bodies pressed together with an electric energy, their breaths mingling and their heartbeats syncing with the other.

As they surrendered to the intense passion that consumed them, time became a distant concept. Their bodies moved in perfect synchronicity, a dance as old as time itself. With every passionate thrust and gasp of pleasure, their souls intertwined, forging an unbreakable bond that transcended their tangled bodies. The room was filled with the scent of sweat and desire, their moans filling the air like a symphony of rapture. They were lost in each other, their senses heightened, completely consumed by the fire that burned between them.

As the moonlight cast a pale glow over the couple in the throes of their passion, a soft breeze blew through the open window, carrying with it a faint whisper of lavender and rose - Odelia's favorite scents. And for a brief moment, John could have sworn he saw her ethereal figure hovering nearby, looking at them with a gentle smile. But instead of feeling heartache, he felt an overwhelming sense of peace. It was like Odelia was giving him her blessing, encouraging him to embrace this.

As they reached the summit of their pleasure, their lovemaking rose to a crescendo, their synchronised moans reverberating off the walls. John and Vivienne locked eyes, their bodies interlocked, and in that moment they knew they had found something special and rare. Amidst the chaos and uncertainty of the world outside, they had created a safe haven within each other's arms, a sanctuary that would guide them through any storms yet to come.

Their bodies, slick with sweat and vibrant paints, collapsed back onto the canvas in a tangle of limbs. The once pristine white surface was now an unbridled scene of passion and connection, every inch marred with smears and splatters of colour. They lay there, breathless and fulfilled, their entwined forms becoming one with the abstract masterpiece beneath them.

John gazed down at Vivienne, his heart swelling with an emotion he had thought lost forever. He traced the contours of her face with a gentle finger, to the beauty beneath the layers of paint. As he moved his hand, he surveyed the canvas beneath them and all its markings.

"Beautiful," he whispered, his voice thick with emotion, moving a curl out of her face.

Vivienne reached up to caress his cheek, her touch as light as a feather. "You know," she murmured. "I've been running from my problems for so long, I'd forgotten what it was like, truly, to connect with another person."

John's mind drifted to Odelia, and for now, the thought of her brought a smile to his lips instead of a stab of pain. "She would have liked you," he said softly. "She always said I needed someone to challenge me, to keep me on my toes."

Vivienne laughed, the sound warm and rich in the room's standoffishness. "I think I would have liked her too," she replied, with an irrepressible smile.

In that slice of time, as they lay cuddled up on the canvas, the evidence of their lovemaking surrounding them, John and Vivienne knew they had found a rare and precious gift. In a world haunted by darkness and despair, they had discovered a glimmer of light within each other.

As the canvas beneath them slowly began to dry, the heat from their bodies and the weight of the thick paint caused it to cling to their skin. They rolled together, as one, until they tumbled onto the bare wooden floor. John's hand grabbed a nearby blanket, pulling it off the sofa and draping it over their enmeshed bodies.

Cocooned in the thickness of the soft blanket, they drifted off to sleep, their bodies still nestled into one another. Contentment was painted across their resting faces, gladly oblivious to the creature observing them - a creature now attached to its victims, torn between good and its very nature, like the fabled scorpion carrying the frog across the river.

CHAPTER 21

But the Bat Crawled Away

Narrator's Note 23.32.1.2 - Regret is the thing with claws, that feasts without pause.

John's eyes slowly fluttered open, the pale morning light searing through the small window of the quaint cottage. As consciousness gradually returned, so did the heavy burden of his actions, dragging down on him like stones in his pockets. The rhythmic sound of Vivienne's gentle breathing beside him rang loud in his ears, each breath serving as a damning reminder of his unforgivable betrayal.

He sat up slowly, the floor creaking beneath his muscular frame. Running a hand through his greying hair, John felt the sting of guilt pierce his heart. How could he have allowed himself to do this?

John paced back and forth in the paint-splattered room, fingers tangled in his hair as he tried to unravel the conflicting emotions that tugged at his heart. The memory of Vivienne's intoxicating scent and seductive touch clouded his mind, but the ghostly presence of Odelia lingered at the edges of his consciousness. He should have known better.

He came to a sudden stop, his bare feet connecting with the icy coldness of the wooden floorboards. The quaint cottage seemed to whisper accusingly, its walls bearing witness to his unfaithfulness. John paced back and forth, his broad shoulders hunched in defeat under the weight of his inner turmoil. Each step echoed through the small space, adding to the heavy atmosphere that clouded around him like a thick fog. The rustic furnishings and warm hues that once brought comfort now felt suffocating in their familiarity. He couldn't escape the overwhelming sense of guilt and regret that consumed him, no matter how hard he tried to shake it off.

"What have I done?" he muttered, his deep voice tinged with anguish. "Odelia, forgive me..."

John's thoughts drifted to his late wife, her memory an ever-present companion in his grief-stricken existence. Odelia had been his guiding light, his anchor in the turbulent sea of life. Her wit and strength had captivated him, binding his heart to hers with an unbreakable bond. Even in death, her presence lingered, a ghostly reminder of the love they once shared.

And yet, here he stood, torn between the past and the present. Vivienne's touch had ignited a fire within him, a fleeting moment of connection in his loneliness. But the flames of desire now gave way to the smouldering embers of regret, the ashes of his loyalty scattered in the wake of his moment of weakness. He knew he shouldn't have let things go this far, but her touch had ignited something within him that he thought had long since died with Odelia.

John's mind raced, seeking a path forward amidst the labyrinth of his conflicted emotions. He knew he could not deny the pull towards Vivienne, the inexplicable connection that seemed to defy the boundaries he so cherished. She deserved to be loved. Without question, without clauses. His head lowered as he came to his regrettable conclusion. They both deserved better.

As he stood there, lost in the depths of his introspection, the cottage seemed to close around him, the weight of his choices bearing down upon his soul. The gothic atmosphere intensified, the shadows deepening as if to echo the darkness that threatened to consume him. John knew he had to find a way forward, to reconcile the warring factions of his heart, but the path ahead seemed shrouded in uncertainty and despair.

John's eyes darted around the room, taking in the remnants of the passion that had transpired between him and Vivienne. The discarded clothing scattered haphazardly across the floor, the rumpled blankets strewn over the bed, and the lingering scent of their intimacy still hung heavily in the air. It was a stark reminder of his disloyalty and betrayal. He couldn't bear to face her, to see the hope and affection in her eyes that he would inevitably crush with his departure.

With a sudden determination, John began to gather his belongings, his movements hurried, hushed, and frantic as if trying to outrun his own guilt. He had to leave, to put distance between himself and the temptation that Vivienne represented. It was the only way he could clear his mind, to find the strength to confront that which haunted him.

As he dressed, John's thoughts raced, his emotions a maelstrom within his chest. He knew his actions would hurt Vivienne, that she would feel abandoned and rejected, but he convinced himself that it was for the best. She deserved someone whole, someone untainted by the scars of loss and grief, and he knew he could never be that man.

With a final glance at Vivienne's sleeping form, John slipped out of the cottage, the door closing behind him with a soft click. The cool morning air hit his face, a stark contrast to the warmth and comfort of the cottage, and he felt a shiver run down his spine. He strode forward, his feet carrying him away from the source of his inner turmoil, each step a silent apology to the woman he was leaving behind.

Vivienne stirred, her hand reaching out instinctively for John's warmth, only to find the space beside her empty and cold. Her eyes fluttered open, confusion and fear gripping her heart as she sat up, the blanket falling away from her bare skin.

She called out his name, her voice echoing, but only silence greeted her in return.

As the realisation of John's absence sank in, Vivienne felt despair wash over her. To find him gone cut through her like a knife, reopening the wounds of her past and intensifying the feelings of worthlessness that had long plagued her. She curled in on herself, her body shaking with silent sobs as the weight of her loneliness consumed her.

The cottage, once feeling something akin to a home, now felt like a prison, the walls closing in around her as she drowned in her sorrow. Vivienne's mind spiralled, the darkness within the house taking hold, whispering cruel truths and taunting her with the futility of her desires. She had dared to hope, to believe, that she could find love and acceptance in John's arms, but now, as she lay alone and broken, she realised the folly of her dreams.

As Vivienne's despair deepened, the creature that lurked within the cottage sensed her vulnerability, its parasitic energy pulsing with anticipation. The air congealed, the temperature dropping to an icy chill that seeped into Vivienne's bones. She shivered, pulling the blanket tighter around her naked form, her breath coming in short, panicked gasps as she felt the unseen force closing in around her.

Out of nowhere, the peaceful stillness was shattered by a cacophony of movement. The furniture seemed to come alive, possessed by some unseen force. The heavy oak dresser suddenly lurched forward, slamming against the wall with a loud crash that echoed through the room. Vivienne's scream pierced the air, her eyes wide with terror as she watched the chaos unfold before her. Knives flew through the air with deadly grace, their sharp blades glinting in the dim light as they narrowly missed her trembling form, embedding themselves in the walls and splintering the wood with a loud crack. The room felt alive with inhuman energy as if it were a puppet being controlled by an unseen master.

"No, no, no," Vivienne whimpered, her voice barely above a whisper as she cowered on the floor, her hands clasped tightly over her ears in a futile attempt to block out the pandemonium. The beast laughed, a cruel, guttural sound that reverberated through the cottage, mocking her fear and relishing in her torment. It sat almost nose-to-nose to her, the putrid odour overpowering, its bright eyes surveying her in curiosity.

With each passing moment, the force grew stronger, feeding off Vivienne's fear and despair like a parasite. The walls shook violently and the floorboards creaked beneath her feet as she tried to stumble away, but there was no escape.

But there was no escape, no respite from the relentless torment that assaulted her senses. Vivienne was trapped, a prisoner in her own personal hell, everything feeding off her fear and despair, growing stronger with each passing moment. She sank to her knees, her body wracked with sobs as she prayed for deliverance, for a glimmer of hope in the darkness that threatened to consume her.

As the lights flickered ominously, casting eerie shadows across the room, Vivienne's fragile state of mind began to crumble under the weight of the force that sought to destroy her. The cottage had become a battleground, where reality blurred with nightmare as the darkness consumed her fragile state of mind. She was trapped in an endless cycle of horror, praying for deliverance that seemed further and further out of reach.

"Why is this happening to me?" she cried out, her voice raw and failing. "What have I done to deserve this?"

The beast remained silent, its stifling energy permeating every corner of the cottage. Vivienne's eyes darted around the room, searching for a way out, but the house moved in on her, suffocating her with their nearness.

With each passing moment, Vivienne's depression deepened, the weight of her despair pressing down upon her like a physical force. She had never felt so utterly hopeless, so completely trapped in a nightmare from which there was no escape. The thought of facing another day, another hour, in this hellish existence was more than she could bear.

"Please, someone help me," she whispered, her voice barely audible above the creaking of the floorboards and the curtains' rustling. But there was no one to hear her pleas, no one to come to her aid in this lonely, forgotten place. John had gone.

The animal watched, its eyes glinting with inquisitiveness as it feasted upon every moment of Vivienne's suffering. It had found the perfect vessel, a fragile, broken woman whose mind was ripe for the taking. And it would not rest until it had claimed her.

As the demonic presence continued its relentless assault, Vivienne found herself cowering in the corner of the cottage, her arms wrapped tightly around her knees as she tried to make herself as small as possible. Objects continued to fly through the air with alarming precision, narrowly missing her head as they shattered against the walls behind her. The very foundations of the cottage seemed to tremble with each impact as if the building itself were crying out in agony.

Vivienne's breath came in short, panicked gasps as she tried to shield herself from the onslaught. "Why?" she cried out, her voice raw with desperation. "What have I done?"

Whispers began to fill her head, insidious thoughts that wormed their way into the deepest recesses of her mind. "You are worthless," they hissed, their voices dripping with venom. "No one could ever love someone as broken and damaged as you. Best leave now."

Vivienne tried to fight against the poisonous words, but they seemed to take root in her, spreading like a cancer until she could no longer distinguish her thoughts from them. She began to believe the lies, to see herself through the twisted lens of the entity that sought to destroy her.

She slumped against the wall, her eyes hollow and unseeing as she gazed into the darkness. Maybe they were right, maybe death was the only escape from this endless torture. She clenched her fist, trying to suppress the sharp pain in her chest as tears streamed down her face. The constant anguish and agony seemed never-ending, but death offered a glimmer of hope for peace and freedom.

Vivienne's sobs echoed through the cottage, each cry a haunting melody of despair. The walls seemed to absorb her anguish, trapping it within the confines of the cursed dwelling. She rocked in the corner, like a child, wanting to disappear from the relentless torment that consumed her.

"End it all," the demon's voice purred, its tone seductive and alluring. "Take the blade and embrace the sweet release of death. It is the only way to escape, to find the peace you so desperately crave."

Vivienne's gaze drifted to the kitchen, where a glint of metal caught her eye. A knife, its edge sharp and inviting, beckoned to her from the counter. She rose slowly as if in a trance, her feet carrying her toward the instrument of her demise.

"Yes, that's it," the demon coaxed, its anticipation growing with each step she took. "One quick slice... and all your suffering will be done."

Vivienne's hand shook uncontrollably as she inched closer to the knife, her fingers trembling as they curled around the solid handle. The metal was frigid against her skin, sending a shiver down her spine and a poignant reminder of the dire situation. With one swift cut, it could all be over. One final surrender to the agonising despair that consumed her every waking moment, and she would find release from this torturous existence. Her breaths came out in ragged gasps, her heart pounding so fiercely she thought it might burst from her chest. The weight of the knife felt heavy in her hand, a symbol of both her desperation and strength in this crucial moment. She took a deep breath, willing herself to make the decision that would ultimately determine her fate.

The sharp, cold edge of the blade pressed against her trembling wrist, leaving a trail of glistening tears in its wake. Vivienne's once bright and lively eyes were now clouded with pain and despair, a shadow of the person she used to be. The presence of evil loomed over her, eagerly anticipating its victory as it watched her every move. With a deep breath, Vivienne closed her eyes and the creature steadied her shaking hand with an oddly comforting stroke of the hair. She was ready to make the final cut that would release her from this endless agony.

CHAPTER 22

I Don't Mind the Rain, But it Won't Wash Me Clean

Narrator's Note 19.9.2.16 - Two steps forward, one step back.

Vivienne stumbled through the moonlit woods, her pale arms covered in angry bruises and jagged scratches, bright red blood mixing with the colourful paint that coated her skin. The once-elegant silk of her dress was now torn and shredded, fluttering behind her like tattered wings. Heart thundering in her chest, she raced towards the solitary glow of John's window, a desperate moth seeking refuge from the shadows nipping at her heels.

As she neared the weathered oak door, Vivienne's trembling hand rasped urgently against the wood. Time slowed, her laboured breathing the only sound aside from the forlorn cry of a distant whip-poor-will. Then, the door creaked open, revealing John's towering form, his green eyes widening as he took in her dishevelled state - her hair wild and tangled, her face streaked with tears and dirt.

"Vivienne! My God, what happened to you?" His voice, usually so controlled, wavered with concern as his gaze swept over her injuries.

Her lips trembled, quivering as she tried to speak. But the words caught in her throat, trapped behind a lump that refused to budge. In that moment, Vivienne longed to surrender herself to John's strong embrace, to feel his solid warmth engulf her and protect her from the nightmares that lurked at every turn. Yet a chasm yawned between them, an abyss she dared not cross uninvited.

John's hand, rough and strong, hovered tentatively in the air just inches from her mottled skin. It was as if he feared she would crumble under his touch, her fragility itself now cumbersome. Vivienne's chest tightened with a deep ache, a tangible manifestation of her yearning for connection, for the solace only he could offer. But just like the phantoms that haunted her, the unspoken ghosts of John's past kept him at arm's length, holding him back from fully giving himself to her.

The seconds ticked by, heavy with unspoken emotions, until he finally stepped aside, a silent invitation. Vivienne crossed the threshold, the floor sighing beneath her bare feet as she left the clinging darkness behind.

As she stood in the foyer, Vivienne's battered body trembled, her strength seeping away like the warmth from her bones. The enormity of her ordeal crashed over her in relentless waves, threatening to drag her beneath the surface. She swayed on her feet, a sapling in the throes of a tornado, until John's steadying hand found the small of her back, a tethered rope in the storm.

"Come, sit," he urged, his deep voice calming her shot nerves. He guided her to the living room, his touch a feather-light pressure against her bruised skin, a reminder of his gentle nature despite his imposing stature.

Vivienne sank into the plush cushions of the velvet sofa, her body sinking into its welcoming embrace. Her mind was consumed by thoughts of escape from the cruel realities that constantly plagued her. John sat down beside her, leaving a respectful distance between them. She could feel his warmth radiating towards her, but she knew he was keeping a barrier between them.

"What happened, Vivienne?" he asked, his emerald eyes searching her face, a mirror of her pain.

She drew a convulsing breath, the air rattling in her lungs like the chains that bound the restless spirits to the mortal plane. "The haunting," she whispered, her voice a threadbare whisper, "it's back. Worse than before."

The words poured from her trembling lips, a torrent of terror and desperation that threatened to consume her. She recounted the events that had driven her from the quaint cottage, each syllable tearing at her throat like jagged glass. The wounds, both physical and emotional, were still raw and festering beneath the surface.

As she spoke, Vivienne felt the weight of her burdens begin to lift, shared now with the one person who understood the depths of her suffering.

In the heavy silence between them, filled with unspoken truths and shared sorrow, Vivienne's gaze drifted to the photographs adorning the walls—snapshots of a life now lost, forever frozen in time. The smiling faces of John and Odelia stared back at her, a cruel reminder of the love and happiness that once filled these rooms. Now, they existed only as ghostly remnants of a distant past. The walls seemed to watch her, suffocating her with memories that she wished fervently to forget.

"I don't belong here," Vivienne murmured like she herself was turning into a ghost. "This was your home, yours and Odelia's. I'm an intruder, a trespasser."

John's brow furrowed. "Vivienne," he began, his voice a low rumble, "you're not—"

But she cut him off, her words tumbling out in a rush as if she feared they might consume her if left unspoken. "I'm broken, John. Damaged. The things I've seen, the horrors I've endured... they've left their mark on me, like a stain that can never be washed clean."

Her voice cracked, the vulnerability in her tone a stark contrast to the steely determination that had driven her for so long. "I fear I'm unlovable, a shattered creature unworthy of affection or compassion. How could anyone want me, knowing what lurks within?"

Vivienne's eyes searched John's face, desperate for a glimmer of understanding, a sign that he recognized the pain that ate at her. She felt stripped bare, her deepest insecurities laid out before him like an offering, a plea for absolution she feared would never come. She tugged at her torn dress, feeling more exposed now than she had done, naked on the floor of the house, only a day ago.

John's gaze softened, the lines of his face seeming to smooth as he regarded her with a mixture of empathy and sorrow. His pain, so long buried beneath a facade of stoic resilience, rose to the surface, etching itself into the contours of his expression.

He swallowed hard as if steeling himself for the words that were to come. "Vivienne, I... I need you to understand something," he began, his voice thick with emotion. "When I left, it wasn't because I didn't care for you. It was because I was afraid."

He paused, his eyes drifting to the window, where the fading light of day cast long shadows across the room. "After Odelia died, I thought I'd never be able to love again. The pain of losing her was like a wound that refused to heal, a constant reminder of the emptiness that had taken root in my heart."

John's gaze returned to Vivienne, his green eyes shimmering with unshed tears. "But then you came into my life, with your fiery spirit and your unwavering determination, and I found myself drawn to you in a way I couldn't explain. And it terrified me, the thought of opening myself up to that kind of pain again."

His voice dropped to a whisper, a confession meant only for her ears. "I pushed you away because I was a coward, too afraid to face the depth of my own feelings."

Vivienne's eyes widened, a mix of surprise and relief washing over her features as she listened to John's words. Her fingers itched with the urge to reach out and brush away the worry lines etched on his forehead, to gently wipe away the tears that threatened to fall from his piercing green eyes. Her heart ached for him, for the pain he had endured and the guilt that had consumed him, and she felt a sudden, overwhelming desire to comfort him, to show him that he was not alone in his suffering.

She extended her hand, fingers trembling slightly as they reached for his. As their skin brushed together, she squeezed his hand gently, a wordless gesture of support and unwavering loyalty. They sat side by side, their hands clasped, speaking without words but understanding each other completely. And in that moment, Vivienne felt a flicker of hope ignite within her, a fragile but persistent reminder that amidst the darkness and uncertainty, there was still the promise of light, love, and a future worth fighting for.

John's voice trembled as he spoke, each word a clue to the turmoil within his heart. "I loved Odelia with every fibre of my being, and losing her shattered me in ways I never thought possible. But you, Vivienne... you've awakened something in me, and it terrifies me because I don't know how to reconcile all these feelings. Big feelings."

He paused, his eyes searching Vivienne's face for any sign of understanding, of acceptance. He felt exposed, vulnerable in a way he had never allowed himself to be before, but there was a strange sense of liberation in finally giving voice to the emotions that had haunted him for so long.

Vivienne's fingers tightened around his, a silent gesture of support and compassion. Her voice was soft, filled with a tenderness that soothed the ragged edges of his soul. "I understand, John. It's intense, whatever this is, and we are complicated. We focus so much on being kind to one another, that we forget to treat ourselves with the same care."

As she spoke, Vivienne felt a wave of empathy wash over her, a deep understanding of the complex emotions that John was grappling with. She knew all too well the pain of loss, the fear of vulnerability, and the hesitance to trust in the possibility of happiness once more.

Vivienne's eyes sparkled with a sudden idea. She leaned forward, her voice carrying a mix of anticipation and vulnerability as she spoke. "John, I have an exhibition of my paintings, coming up next week. It would mean the world to me if you could be there, to see the art that has been my solace and escape during these trying times. I know it's a lot to ask, but I feel like.. this... we can manage. Big feelings or not."

John's brow furrowed, his green eyes searching Vivienne's face as he wrestled with the invitation. Slowly, hesitantly,

John's lips curved into a smile, a tentative expression that held the promise of healing and discovery. "I would be honoured to attend your exhibition, Vivienne. I know it takes courage to share your art with the world, to lay bare your soul for others to see."

He looked at her almost pityingly, her trembling not subsiding at all. "You mustn't go back to that house tonight, it's not safe. Stay here. Please. Big feelings or not."

CHAPTER 23

Bathtubs and Brooding

Narrator's Note 20.26.2.8 - Trauma does strange things to people, it simultaneously makes them old beyond their years in some ways and immensely child-like in others.

John's footsteps echoed through the dimly lit hallway as he led Vivienne towards the bedroom, his broad shoulders casting long shadows on the faded wallpaper. A solemn expression formed deep lines into his weathered face, his grief mingling with concern for the trembling woman at his side. He paused at the entrance, his large hand resting on the brass doorknob.

"You'll be safe here, Vivienne," he said with a reassuring rumble. "I promise no harm will come to you under my watch."

Vivienne's heart fluttered as she met John's intense green gaze, finding a flicker of warmth amidst the sadness that clouded his eyes. She hesitated, fear still clawing at her insides, the memory of the creature at the cottage an icy whisper down her spine. But exhaustion tugged at her heavy limbs, everything taking its toll.

With a trembling breath, Vivienne entered the bedroom, the atmosphere heavy with the sweet aroma of lavender and the musty smell of old books. The massive four-poster bed dominated the space, its sturdy wooden frame decorated with delicate carvings of blooming roses, now faded and worn from years of use. She lowered herself onto the plush mattress, relieved to feel its coolness against her burning skin. As she moved, flakes of dried paint crumbled off her body and onto the pristine white sheets, but John paid it no mind.

His gaze never wavered as Vivienne curled into herself, her delicate hands clutching the sheets with a white-knuckled grip. She looked like a fragile flower, one that had been trampled and left to wilt. He couldn't help but feel a surge of protectiveness towards her, a fierce desire to shield her from the dark demons that plagued her mind. He longed to wrap her in his arms and hold her close, whispering soothing words until the nightmares faded away. But for now, all he could do was watch and hope that his presence alone would bring her some small comfort and security.

"Rest now," he murmured, his voice a gentle caress. "I'll be right outside if you need me."

As John turned to leave, Vivienne's whisper reached his ears. "Thank you, John."

He paused, his heart constricting with a bittersweet ache. In that moment, he saw something of his beloved Odelia in Vivienne's eyes – the same vulnerability, the same plea for sanctuary from the cruelties of the world. Throat tight with emotion, John could only nod before quietly closing the door behind him.

In the solitude of the bedroom, Vivienne allowed tears to fall, silent rivulets cascading down her pale cheeks. Her fears, the gnawing dread that had consumed her for so long, poured out in a torrent of anguish. She prayed for a dreamless sleep, a respite from the nightmares that clawed at her mind.

John trudged his way to the living room, each step heavy against the creaking hardwood floor. The once familiar house now felt desolate, an empty shell that echoed with the absence of his beloved wife. He paused by the sturdy sofa, its worn fabric sagging under the weight of countless memories. His gaze fell upon the thin blanket draped over its back, a bittersweet reminder of nights spent snuggled together with Odelia.

He let out a mirthless chuckle as he ran his hand over the faded fabric, recalling all the times they had wrapped themselves in it while watching their favorite movies or simply enjoying each other's company. With a weary sigh, John sank onto the soft cushions, pulling the cherished blanket close to his chest. It was tattered and worn, much like his heart after losing Odelia. He closed his eyes and breathed deeply, hoping to catch a faint trace of her perfume, but only finding the musty smell of disuse.

In the bedroom upstairs, Vivienne tossed and turned, the crisp white sheets tangled around her limbs like a desperate grasp for safety. Her brow furrowed in distress as she fought against the unseen demons that haunted her dreams. Whimpers of fear escaped her trembling lips, punctuating the heavy silence of the night like a haunting melody.

In her mind's eye, Vivienne found herself back at the quaint cottage, the darkness of night closing in around her like a sinister embrace. The air was thick with an ominous energy, sending chills down her spine. She tried to run, but her feet remained rooted as if held captive by an invisible force.

The nightmare shifted, and suddenly Vivienne was stood before a cracked mirror, its reflection distorted and grotesque. Eyes black as coal glared back at her from the twisted image, a wicked grin stretching across its face. The reflection reached out with long, bony fingers towards Vivienne, its touch cold and clammy against her skin. She could feel its grip pulling her closer and closer until she was almost consumed by the dark being.

Vivienne's scream shattered the quiet of the night, jolting John from his reverie in an instant. His heart raced as he bolted into action, racing up the stairs with determined footsteps. Bursting into the bedroom, he found Vivienne thrashing on the bed, her face contorted in pure terror like an effect in a house of mirrors.

Without hesitation, John gathered her into his arms, cradling her trembling form against his chest. "Shh, it's okay," he murmured, his voice a soothing balm to her frayed nerves. "I'm here. You're safe now."

Vivienne clung to him, her tears soaking into the fabric of his shirt. In the safety of John's embrace, the nightmares began to recede, replaced by a fragile sense of peace.

He could still see Odelia's face everywhere, her spark forever etched into him. The way her silver hair cascaded down her back, the mischievous glint in her eyes when she teased him, the gentle curve of her lips when she smiled - every detail was a bittersweet reminder of what he had lost.

The silence that followed was suffocating, broken only by the soft ticking of the antique clock on the mantelpiece. John closed his eyes, allowing the memories to wash over him like a tidal wave. He remembered the day they first met, the electricity that crackled between them, the way her laughter filled the room and made his heart skip a beat. He remembered their wedding day, the way she glided down the aisle like an angel, the love that shone in her eyes as she pledged her life to him.

In the bedroom, Vivienne's breathing grew shallow and uneven, her fear intensifying with each passing moment. The nightmares that plagued her were relentless, their icy tendrils snaking into the deepest recesses of her mind. She clutched at him, her knuckles turning white as she fought against the unseen forces that threatened to consume her.

Her distress echoed through the house, mingling with the wind. John's heart ached for her, for the trauma that she endured, for the darkness that haunted her every waking moment. He longed to take away her pain, to shield her from the horrors that lurked in the shadows.

As he sat alone in the dimly lit room, his mind was filled with memories of Odelia. He closed his eyes and felt the weight of guilt pressing down on him, suffocating him. The constant replay of her death haunted him, a constant reminder of his shortcomings. And now, as he looked at Vivienne sleeping peacefully beside him, he couldn't help but feel a surge of fear and helplessness. He didn't want to fail her like he failed Odelia.

As she began to settle, he tucked her back into bed with the utmost care, as though she were a fragile piece of blown glass. His hands moved delicately, like a skilled artist shaping a masterpiece. He planted a soft kiss on her forehead and then tiptoed out of the room, closing the door with the faintest of sounds. It was as if he didn't want to disturb the peaceful atmosphere surrounding her, like a protective blanket shielding her from the outside world. He left her room feeling content, knowing that she was safe and sound in her own little haven.

John's footsteps echoed through the hallway and dimly lit living room as he paced back and forth, his mind a tumultitude of thoughts. The moonlight cast an eerie glow through the window, painting the room in shades of silver and shadow. He paused by the window, his eyes drawn to the landscape beyond, a vast expanse of darkness broken only by the ghostly shimmer of the moon on the distant waves.

The emptiness within him seemed to mirror the desolate beauty of the night. The loss of Odelia had left a gaping void in his soul, a wound that refused to heal. He closed his eyes, his fingers pressing against the cool glass as if seeking a connection to something beyond the confines of his pain.

"Odelia," he whispered, his voice a mere echo. "I'm lost without you."

The silence that followed was deafening, a stark reminder of the absence that haunted him. He felt the weight of his guilt pressing down upon him, the knowledge that he had failed her in her final moments. If only he had been there... if only he had seen the signs...

A blood-curdling scream shattered the silence for a second time, echoing through the empty hallway. His heart pounded as he recognized the voice, the unmistakable terror that laced every syllable. It was Vivienne.

Without a second thought, he raced up the stairs, his long strides carrying him to their bedroom in mere seconds. He burst through the door, his eyes wide with fear and concern as he took in the scene before him.

Vivienne, now fully awake, sat upright in bed, her body trembling violently as if she were caught in the grip of some unseen force. Her once smooth skin was now glistening with a thin layer of sweat, giving her an otherworldly glow. Her eyes were wild and frantic, haunted by the vivid images that had torn her from sleep. She clutched at her chest, her fingers digging into her nightgown as if trying to anchor herself back to reality. Every breath came out in ragged gasps, the air stolen from her lungs.

"Vivienne," John said softly, approaching the bed with cautious steps. "It's okay. Safe space."

But even as the words left his lips, he knew they were a hollow comfort. The demons that haunted her were not so easily banished, and the scars they left were not so easily healed.

Vivienne's gaze met his, her eyes filled with a desperate plea for help, for understanding. "I can't escape it, John. The darkness, the evil... it's always there, waiting for me. I can feel it, even now, lurking in the shadows."

John sat down on the edge of the bed, his hand reaching out to gently brush away the tears that streamed down her face. "I know," he whispered, his voice heavy with empathy. "But you're not alone, Vivienne. I'm here. I won't let it take you."

Even as he spoke the words, he felt the weight of his doubts, his fears. How could he protect her from the unseen horrors that stalked her dreams, when he was so lost in his own darkness?

Vivienne's grip on John's arm tightened, her fingers digging into his skin with a desperate intensity. "I can't go back there alone, John. The cottage... it's cursed. Every time I close my eyes, I see it. The shadows, the whispers, the cold touch of something evil." Her voice trembled, each word a fragile confession of the terror that consumed her.

He drew her closer, his arms encircling her like a shield against the unseen horrors that haunted her. "We'll find a way to get rid of it, Vivienne. I promise you. I won't let you face this alone."

She looked down at the powdery, sweaty mess she had become, itching and scratching like mad. "Sorry" she said slowly.

"Not at all. Let me get you cleaned up."

He disappeared into the bathroom, the running water echoing from inside. After a few minutes, he emerged, steam billowing behind him, being careful to make no sudden movements.

With gentle strength, John scooped Vivienne into his arms, cradling her trembling form against his chest. He carried her to the bathroom, the soft glow of the skylight casting flickering shadows on the walls. The air was fragrant with orange blossom, a feeble attempt to mask the pervasive darkness that seemed to seep into every corner of the room.

John tenderly lowered Vivienne into the awaiting bath, the warm water caressing her body like a comforting hug. She clung to him with all of her might, her fingers tightly gripping his shoulders, her chest rising and falling rapidly. The steam rising from the water filled the room with a cozy warmth, enveloping them in a cocoon of relaxation. Vivienne's tired muscles sighed in relief as she sunk deeper into the comforting embrace of the bath.

"I've got you," John murmured, his voice a deep rumble that seemed to resonate through her very bones. "You're safe here, with me."

With a gentle tug, he slid her ruined dress over her head and tossed it aside, revealing her bare skin. Reaching for the sponge, he dipped it into the warm water and wiped it over her, careful not to apply too much pressure. The grime and grime and grunge slowly melted away under his touch, something of herself returning. The simple act of bathing her, of tending to her in this moment of vulnerability, stirred something within him.

But even as he washed away the physical remnants of her fear, he knew that the true battle lay within. The demons that plagued her mind, the ghosts of her past that refused to be silenced... those were the enemies he couldn't simply wash away.

As John gently guided her out of the warm bath, he wrapped her in a plush towel, feeling the softness of the fabric against his skin. Holding her close, he could sense her finding her balance, her steps becoming more confident and steady.

"Steady as she goes," he whispered to reassure her, getting a tired smile in response.

The night wore on, the shadows in the room seeming to lengthen with each passing hour. Vivienne lay curled on the bed, her body still, save for the occasional twitch or whimper that escaped her lips. John sat beside her, his hand resting gently on her shoulder, a silent reminder that she was not alone.

Vivienne's breath hitched, her brow furrowing as she fought against the nightmares that plagued her. John leaned closer, his voice low and soothing as he whispered words of comfort. "All a dream."

She stirred, her eyes fluttering open momentarily, glassy and unfocused. "John?" Her voice was small and sleepy.

"I'm here," he murmured, brushing a stray curl from her forehead. "Rest now. I'll keep watch."

She nodded, her eyes drifting shut once more as exhaustion claimed her. John settled back in his chair, his gaze never leaving her face.

Beneath that delicate exterior, he knew, lay a strength that even she had yet to fully understand. A resilience that had carried her through the darkest of times, that had brought her to his doorstep in search of salvation.

For, in the end, it was all they had left. Each other, and the hope that somehow, someday, they would work it all out.

CHAPTER 24

Her Name was Vivienne, it Never Suited Her

Narrator's Note 22.14.4.21 - Fun is not solely a child's vocation.

The imposing stone edifice of Loftus Town Hall loomed before John as he stepped from his car into the gathering dusk. His pulse quickened a strange mingling of anticipation and melancholy pride swelling in his chest as he approached the arched entrance. He had been back to the cottage with Vivienne to collect her paintings, but she wouldn't let him see.

"You're not getting spoilers," she had said teasingly.

Inside, the vaulted atrium hummed with the cultivated chatter of the art aficionados who had come to admire Vivienne's exhibition. John moved slowly through the crowd, feeling oddly separated, a lurking shadow amidst the lively throng. His eyes roamed over the vibrant canvases adorning the walls, each a window into Vivienne's turbulent soul - riotous explosions of colour and raw emotion that stirred something deep within him.

"Mr Bassinger, so glad you could join us this evening." A woman's voice, rich and melodious, drew his attention. John turned to see the curator, Evelyn Blackwood, her raven hair swept into an elegant chignon, her eyes gleaming like polished onyx.

"Ms. Blackwood." He inclined his head politely. "I wouldn't have missed it. Vivienne's talent deserves to be celebrated."

"Indeed. Her work is quite...provocative, wouldn't you say?" Evelyn's scarlet lips curved in a knowing smile. "I imagine it resonates with you on a profoundly personal level, given your shared history."

John felt a pang, memories of loss and longing threatening to engulf him. He fought to maintain his composure, his jaw tightening imperceptibly. "Her art speaks to the human condition in all its complexity. It's a rare gift."

Evelyn studied him for a long moment, her gaze penetrating. "Of course. Well, do enjoy the exhibition. I suspect you may find some of the pieces particularly...moving." With that, she glided away, vanishing into the crowd like a wisp of smoke.

John stood opposite a painting, hands on hips, staring pensively at the shock of colour. The gallery was quiet except for the sound of his heavy breathing. Memories flooded his mind as he gazed at the artwork - memories of his lost love, his mistakes, and the pain that never seemed to leave. He closed his eyes momentarily, trying to calm himself before resuming his slow walk around the exhibit, steeling himself to feel once again.

Each painting he passed seemed to capture a fragment of the fractured soul - stormy seascapes, twisted figures wreathed in shadow, desolate landscapes that mirrored the barren wasteland of his own heart. And yet, amidst the darkness, there were flashes of light - a single pale rose blooming in a garden of thorns, a shaft of sunlight piercing a leaden sky. Glimpses of hope, fragile and fleeting, yet somehow all the more precious for their rarity.

"There is beauty in the brokenness if one only has the courage to see it." The words drifted through John's mind, an echo of something Vivienne had once said to him. He felt a sudden, fierce rush of pride for all she had overcome, all she had achieved in the face of such adversity.

His gaze lingered on a canvas depicting a figure kneeling in a field of ashes, face uplifted to a blood-red sky. The image seemed to reach into the depths of his being, stirring the embers of suppressed emotions. For a moment, he could almost feel the heat of the flames, taste the bitter ashes on his tongue.

"Oh, Vivienne," he murmured, his voice scarcely more than a whisper. "What you've captured here...it's a revelation."

John's steps faltered as he inched closer to another painting, a sudden and overwhelming realisation washing over him like a tsunami. It was the very same canvas they had made love upon - their bodies tangled in an intense and fiery embrace, surrendering to the all-consuming passion that left them both breathless. Immediately, the memory of that night seared into his mind with vivid clarity - the feel of Vivienne's supple skin beneath his fingers, the way her eyes glittered with desire in the flickering candlelight, the intoxicating taste of her lips pressed against his own. Every fibre of his being yearned to reach out and touch the paint, to relive the passion that still burns within him after all this time.

He stood transfixed, his heart pounding as he gazed upon the artwork they had made. The image seemed to dance before his eyes, as he nervously traced the shapes, the rest of the world fell away, and there was only the painting, and the bittersweet ache of remembrance.

"I remember," John whispered, his fingers hovering just above the surface of the canvas, not quite daring to touch. "How could I ever forget?"

The memory was a double-edged sword, as sweet as it was painful. It reminded him of all he had lost, all he could never reclaim. And yet, there was a strange sort of solace in it, too - a reminder that even in the darkest times, there could still be moments of transcendent beauty.

A sharp sting caused his eyes to water, but he stubbornly blinked away the tears, refusing to let his emotions take control of him in this public setting. Instead, he inhaled deeply, taking in the familiar scent of oil paint and turpentine around him, grounding him in the present moment. The pungent aroma filled his nostrils and brought back memories of immeasurable time spent in the cottage, with these very same materials.

As John struggled to regain his composure, Vivienne glided through the crowd towards him, her lips curved in a playful smirk. The mischievous glint in her eyes sent a shiver across his body, and he found himself torn between the desire to flee and the overwhelming urge to pull her into his arms.

"I see you've found our little masterpiece," she purred, her voice low and intimate. "What do you think, John? Does it do justice to the memory?"

He swallowed hard, his mouth suddenly dry. "It's... it's perfect, Viv. But I don't understand. Why would you put something so private on display for all the world to see?"

Vivienne's smile softened as she watched scarlet creep up his face, and she brushed her fingertips along his jaw. "Because, my darling, art is meant to be shared. And what could be more beautiful?"

John's heart clenched at her words, and he found himself leaning into her touch, craving the warmth of her skin against his own. "But what will people think? What will they say?"

"They won't know, and even if they do, let them talk," Vivienne murmured, her eyes sparkling with naughtiness. "Their opinions are of no consequence."

John couldn't help but smile at her boldness, her utter lack of concern at anyone's judgement.

His heart raced as Vivienne leaned in closer, her breath tickling his ear. "Just imagine," she whispered, her voice low and sultry, "this painting, hanging in your house."

He swallowed hard, his mind flooded with images of tangled limbs and sweat-slicked skin, of desperate gasps and whispered promises in the dark. It was a temptation he couldn't resist, a siren song that called to him from the depths of his very soul.

Slowly, tentatively, he reached out and took her hand in his, fingers intertwining, like two halves of a whole. "O..o...okay," he stuttered. "I'll take it. The painting, I mean."

Vivienne's smile was radiant, her eyes shining with a joy that took his breath away. "It's not all that's on offer," she murmured, brushing her lips against his cheek. "I'm yours, John."

John straightened his tie and smoothed down his hair before approaching the curator, her read of him earlier intimidating him. He felt a knot of nerves in his stomach as he went to speak, her eyes already sizing him up.

"Excuse me," he said, his deep voice resonating with determination, "I'd like to purchase the painting titled 'Heaven's Gate.'"

The curator's eyes widened slightly, a knowing smile playing at the corners of her lips. "Ah, yes. A stunning piece, isn't it?" She studied John for a moment. "She said you'd be interested."

John nodded, his gaze drifting back to the canvas that had captured his heart. "It's meaningful," he admitted, his voice barely above a whisper.

Evelyn's expression softened, understanding in her eyes. "Art has a way of speaking to us on a profound level," she mused, her fingers brushing lightly against the painting's frame."

"I'll take it," he said, his voice firm and resolute. "Whatever the price, it's worth it."

Evelyn nodded with a satisfied smile on her face. "Very well. I'll have it wrapped and ready for you in just a moment." She paused, her gaze meeting John's once more.

With those parting words, Evelyn disappeared into the back room in search of wrapping, leaving John alone with his thoughts. He turned back to the painting, his fingers tracing the delicate strokes that had brought his and Vivienne's moment of passion to life. And in that instant, he knew he was ready to take a chance, to open his heart to the possibility of love once more.

John watched as Evelyn carefully wrapped the painting in layers of protective packaging, her movements precise and deliberate. Each fold of the paper felt like a promise, a guarantee the intimate moment captured on the canvas would be preserved for eternity. With every passing second, John's anticipation grew, his heart pounding as he imagined the painting hanging in his home, a constant reminder of the connection he shared with Vivienne.

John's fingers curled around the edges of the package, as Evelyn handed it to him, holding it close to his chest as he made his way towards the exit. The bustling crowd of the exhibition faded into the background, their voices and laughter becoming nothing more than a distant hum. In that moment, all that mattered was the painting and the memories it held.

As he stepped out into the cool evening air, John felt a sense of peace. The grief that had once consumed his every waking moment seemed to have lost its hold, replaced by a quiet sense of contentment. He had supported Vivienne's talent and had shown her that he believed in her and the beauty she brought into the world. And in doing so, he had taken a step toward healing his wounded heart.

The streets of Loftus were quiet, the only sound was the distant rumble of traffic and the soft rustling of leaves in the wind. John walked with purpose, his strides long and confident as he went to his car. The painting was a comforting weight in his arms, a reminder that even in the darkest of times, there was still hope to be found.

As he drove home, John's mind wandered to the future, to the possibilities that lay ahead. The painting was just the beginning, a small but significant step towards a life filled with love and purpose. And though the road ahead was sure to be filled with challenges and obstacles, John knew he was ready to face them head-on, armed with the knowledge that he was no longer alone.

The drive home seemed to pass in a blur, the streetlights casting a warm glow over the quiet neighbourhood. As John pulled into his driveway, he felt anticipation building in his chest, a fluttering of excitement that he hadn't felt in a long time.

John walked through the front door with the treasured package tucked under his arm, setting it down gently on the kitchen table. He pulled back the protective wrapping, his breath catching in his throat as he took in the vibrant colours and bold shapes. He couldn't help but smile as he took in the familiar shapes and outlines of Vivienne's body within the abstract design. It was even more beautiful than he remembered. Lost in thought, he traced his fingers over the painting, feeling a mix of emotions stirring within him.

He set about finding the perfect spot to display the painting. He moved through the house with a critical eye, considering each wall and corner with care. Finally, he settled on a spot in the living room, a blank stretch of wall that seemed to be waiting for just such a piece.

As he hung the painting, John felt a sense of rightness settle over him, a feeling that he was exactly where he was meant to be.

As he stepped back to admire his handiwork, John knew that no matter what was next, he would face it with a renewed sense of hope and purpose. There, surrounded by the beauty and love that Vivienne had brought into his life, anything seemed possible. All encapsulated in a single painting.

"It's beautiful, isn't it?" A familiar voice whispered behind him.

John turned to see Odelia at his shoulder, her translucent form floating just inches from the ground. Her pale dress rippled as if water, and her eyes sparkled.

"It is," John agreed, his voice thick with emotion.

Odelia's eyes softened, and she reached out to touch John's cheek. He felt the icy chill of her ghostly fingers, but he leaned into the touch all the same, her form disintegrating on contact.

With that, Odelia faded away, leaving John alone once more. But he didn't feel alone, not really. He could still feel her presence, could still hear her words echoing in his mind.

CHAPTER 25

Talk

Narrator's Note 20.3.2.4 - Home is not merely the house lived in.

John stood before the full-length mirror, his tall figure towering over the reflection. He straightened his black silk tie with unsteady fingers, trying to calm his nerves before the big meeting. The richness of his charcoal suit hugged his broad shoulders and lean frame perfectly, but he couldn't shake off the feeling of vulnerability it brought. Taking a deep breath, he anxiously checked his appearance one last time. It felt like he was getting ready for a first date, albeit an unconventional one.

Across town, Vivienne stood in front of her own lavish bedroom mirror. She gently smoothed the folds of her burgundy silk dress, savoring its luxurious feel against her skin. It was a gift from John, tailored to accentuate her curves and give her an air of regal beauty. As she moved, the material swirled elegantly around her feet, making her feel like a goddess. A dainty gold necklace adorned her neck, with a small stag pendant that John had given her as a symbol of their love. She smiled, knowing how much thought he had put into every detail for tonight's special occasion.

Before venturing into the night, Vivienne took a final look at herself in the mirror, ensuring every detail of her appearance was perfect. She wrapped a delicate black lace shawl around her shoulders, its intricate floral patterns serving as a fashion statement and a shield against the looming darkness. As she stepped from the dirt track onto the cobblestone path, her heels clicked rhythmically against the ancient stones, echoing through the quiet streets like a secret signal.

As she walked down the path towards him, John's face lit up like a sunrise. His eyes were filled with pride and admiration as he took her hand and spun her around, admiring her beauty. He leaned in and placed a gentle kiss on the back of her hand, setting off butterflies in her abdomen.

"Incomparable," he let out a deep, satisfied sigh.

"As are you," she said sheepishly, her cheeks flushing. "And thank you for these, they're beautiful."

"As are you," he smirked as he repeated her words back to her.

As they stepped out into the darkening streets, John clasped Vivienne's hand and felt a surge of hope. They had been through so much together, but their love had only grown stronger. The streetlights flickered on, casting eerie observers on the pavement as they walked towards their apartment. As they turned the corner, a gust of wind blew through, causing the leaves to rustle and sending a chill down their spines. But they held onto each other, determined to face whatever challenges lay ahead as long as they were together.

The restaurant loomed before them like a gothic castle, its towering stone walls shrouded in shadows. Wrought iron sconces flickered with an eerie glow, casting dancing shadows across the weathered facade. John and Vivienne ascended the steps, each creaking under their weight as they approached the heavy oak door. With a loud groan, it swung open, revealing a realm of haunting elegance within.

As they stepped inside, the atmosphere weighed heavily on their shoulders. The scent of aged wood and burning enveloped them, transporting them to another time. The dim lighting, provided by strategically placed sconces, cast a spectral light across every corner of the room. Rich velvet draperies hung from the walls, while intricately carved mahogany panels adorned the ceiling above. It was like stepping into a forgotten era, filled with opulence and intrigue.

A sombre-looking waiter, his face a mask of quiet solemnity, approached them with a bow. "Welcome," he intoned, his voice a hushed whisper. "Please, allow me to escort you to your table."

John placed a gentle hand on the small of Vivienne's back, a silent gesture of reassurance as they followed the waiter through the labyrinthine dining room. The flickering candlelight danced across the tables, casting a mesmerising play of light and shadow across the faces of the diners, their expressions a mix of reverence and unease.

As they were led deeper into the maze-like interior, Vivienne couldn't shake the feeling of being watched. She shivered and instinctively moved closer to John, who squeezed her hand reassuringly.

Finally, they reached their destination - a secluded corner of the restaurant, tucked away from prying eyes. The candlelit table was set with gleaming silver and delicate china, and a bouquet of vibrant flowers served as a centerpiece. John pulled out Vivienne's chair like a true gentleman, eliciting a small smile from her.

As they settled into their seats, the waiter lit the candle at the centre of the table. Its dancing flame cast an intimate glow across their faces, blocking out any lingering fears or doubts.

The waiter presented them with leather-bound menus, the pages heavy with the weight of culinary mysteries waiting to be unravelled. As they perused the offerings, tantalising aromas began to waft from the kitchen, enticing their senses with promises of gastronomic delights.

John's eyes scanned the menu, his brow furrowed in concentration. "The braised lamb shank looks tempting," he mused, his voice low and contemplative. "Though I find myself drawn to the steak."

Vivienne nodded, her gaze lingering on the pages. "I understand," she replied, her voice barely above a whisper. "Easy eating."

As they made their selections, the aroma of searing meat and fragrant herbs grew stronger, a symphony of scents dancing around them, heightening their anticipation for the meal to come. Now, the simplicity of ordering dinner felt like a sacred ritual, a prelude to the battles ahead.

John leaned forward, his eyes intense in the candlelight. "Vivienne," he began, his voice heavy. "We need to discuss our plans for the cottage."

Vivienne met his gaze, her own eyes shimmering with a mixture of determination and fear. "I know," she whispered, her fingers unconsciously tracing the edge of her napkin. "It's a daunting task."

John reached across the table, his hand finding hers, their fingers intertwining in a silent gesture of support. "I won't lie to you," he said, his voice raw with emotion. "I'm afraid of what we might encounter, of the horrors that await us. But I also know that we have no choice. We must confront this evil, for the sake of our sanity, and for the memory of those we've lost."

Vivienne nodded, her grip tightening on his hand. "I share your fears, John," she confessed, trembling slightly. "But I also share your resolve."

As they sat there, hands clasped, eyes locked, the candlelight casting shadows across their faces, John and Vivienne knew that they were no longer just two individuals, but rather two halves of a whole united in their determination to face the darkness that threatened to consume them. Amidst the gothic splendour of the restaurant, they found strength in each other, a glimmer of hope in the face of the unknown.

John's thumb gently caressed the back of Vivienne's hand, a small gesture of comfort and reassurance. He leaned forward, his voice low and earnest. "I know we've both suffered, Vivienne. We've both experienced pain and loss that no one should ever have to endure. But I want you to know that you're not alone in this. I'm here with you, every step of the way."

"Are you ready to order?" The waiter startled them out of their conversation.

"Certainly. Viv?" John gestured for her to go first, his eyes still scrutinising the menu.

"Oooh, can I get the prawn cocktail to start, please? And for main... you know what I think I'll have a hot shot parmo! Thank you." Vivienne smiled as she handed back the menu.

"And for you, sir?"

"Could I also get the prawn cocktail to start? But then for main, I'll go for the mushroom stroganoff with potatoes please." John closed the menu with a thud. "And could we get a bottle of house red and two glasses? Thank you so much."

The waiter breezed off, returning momentarily with the wine before attending to other guests.

John reached back across the table, his hand gently covering Vivienne's. The warmth of his touch sent a shiver down her spine, a reminder of the growing connection between them. "Vivienne, I know we've both been through hell. I know I've disappeared a couple of times but no more. I feel like we can talk our way through anything now."

Vivienne looked into John's eyes, seeing the sincerity and the determination that burned within them. She knew that he meant every word, that he truly believed in their ability to triumph over the darkness that threatened to engulf them. And in that moment, she felt a flicker of something else, something that she hadn't felt in a long time: hope.

The waiter set down their meals with a smile, waiting for confirmation that all was well before he sashayed away.

"I disappeared a couple of times too. We can do this. We have to stand firm. Big feelings or not."

John squeezed her hand, his gaze never wavering. "We go in, we name them and we tell them to leave. Then we stay."

Vivienne inhaled deeply, filling her lungs with the fresh autumn air. John's voice wrapped around her like a comforting blanket as he spoke, urging her to push past their doubts and fears. She nodded, feeling determination swell within her. Together, they would conquer their inner demons and emerge stronger.

"You're right, my darling. The things that haunt us shouldn't stop us from living."

The lingering aroma of their meal still hung in the air as John and Vivienne savoured the final bites. The gentle hum of conversation and clinking of silverware filled the restaurant, a warm and inviting atmosphere. Suddenly, a strong gust of wind swept through the dining room, causing the candles on their table to flicker and extinguish. The once cosy ambience was now replaced with momentary darkness, shadows twisting and writhing in the low light.

But John and Vivienne were not intimidated by this ominous omen. They shared a knowing look, silently acknowledging the looming danger. They had been preparing for this battle against the demonic presence, and they knew it was now drawing closer.

Despite the chill that ran down their spines, they refused to let fear dampen their spirits. They had come too far, fought too hard, to let a mere gust of wind deter them from their chosen path. With a determined nod, John signalled for the bill, eager to leave the safety of the restaurant and face whatever challenges lay ahead with unwavering bravery.

As they stepped out into the night, the cool air kissed their skin, a stark contrast to the warm, intimate atmosphere of the restaurant. John's arm instinctively wrapped around Vivienne's waist, pulling her close as they walked down the dimly lit street, their steps syncing.

They knew now what they had to do.

CHAPTER 26

Some Walls are Meant to Tumble Down

Narrator's Note 24.30.1.10 - It is easy to forget your own advice.

J ohn's hand trembled as he turned the old, rusted door knob and pushed open the wooden door. He felt Vivienne's steady grip on his arm as they stepped inside, the musty smell of damp wood filling their nostrils. The air in the cottage was heavy and stifling, like a thick blanket pressing down on them. John could feel the creature still resting within these walls, an intangible presence that seemed to whisper and creep around them. Cold sweat beaded on his forehead as he took a shaky step forward, the squeaky floor accompanying the house's eerie atmosphere.

"Do you feel that?" Vivienne whispered, her voice barely audible above the deafening silence. "It's like the walls are watching us, waiting for the right moment to strike."

John's jaw clenched tightly, his muscles straining against the suffocating atmosphere wrapped around them. He could see the sinister presence lurking in the shadows, its penetrating gaze fixated on them. Every inhale felt like a struggle against its diabolical power, and he could sense the evil intent emanating from it, hairs standing on end.

"Stay close," John murmured, his voice low and urgent. "We don't know what we're dealing with here."

Vivienne's slender hand slipped effortlessly into his, her warm touch reflexively making him soften. Her delicate fingers intertwined with his own in an unyielding grip, providing with with a sense of security that he had never really known before, in that way.

As they ventured deeper into the abandoned cottage, John could feel the beast creeping ever closer, stalking its prey. The air around them grew darker, trying to limit their vision and keep them from moving forward. Every bone in their collective bodies was screaming to run, but they knew what was at stake. They had to stay.

Despite the rotting wood and decaying smell, John couldn't help but enjoy the haunting beauty of the perenially dilapidated structure. Though both Vivienne and John had made good progress, the house still shook off any attempt to change it. The only evidence of any acceptance were Vivienne's gorgeous murals, glinting like jewels in the sun. For the rest of the house, the peeling wallpaper revealed intricate designs of twisted vines and thorns, while cobwebs clung to every surface like sinister strings. And the creature seemed quite contented about that.

But this journey was not just about exploring an old building - it was a battle against pure evil. Whispers and shrieks echoed through the corridors, desperately trying to to intimidate them into turning back. A giggle of a child, a movement of a piece of furniture, a memory played out in real-time, the house kept humbly testing their boundaries.

Their love served as an impenetrable shield against the forces of darkness, neither of them once considering they would turn back around. The room started to shake and Vivienne slipped, almost falling to the floor. The house would resort to violence before long, but in the pockets of renewal they had managed to keep, it seemed less inclined to fight.

And so they pressed on, their footsteps echoing through the eerie silence sa they braved whatever horrors showed themselves. But with their love as their guiding light, they were fearless in the face of uncertainty and ready to confron whatever awaited them in the shadows.

The heavy wooden doors slammed shut behind them with a resounding thud, the noise echoing through the small cottage like a death knell. John's heart leaped into his throat, his pulse racing as he spun around, his eyes wide with fear. The ancient woodscreamed, protesting the couple's very presence in this cursed place. The very walls of the cottage were alive, an extension of the creature's power, pulsing with inhuman energy that sent shivers down John's spine. The house was warning them to leave before it was too late, an act of mercy it should have proffered days ago.

Vivienne's grip on his hand tightened, her nails digging into his skin. "John," she whispered, her voice trembling, "we're trapped."

John's throat tightened as her desperately scanned their surroundings. Their only chance for escape was blocked, and their decision to stay now a permanent one. Shadows slinked along the walls, twisting and contorting like suffering souls, their movements wild and unpredictable. They had eyes that mirrored that of the beast, as if the house and its innards had been its creation. The force ravaged them, pulling them apart from one another. With a final surge, John and Vivienne were violently ripped away from each other, imprisoned in separate rooms within the dark and twisted house.

Their nightmare had only just begun.

"VIVIENNE!"

"JOHN! JOHN!"

John pounded on the door with his fists, kicking and shouting.

And then, from the corner of his eye, John caught a glimpse of something that made his blood run cold. A figure, ethereal and glowing, stood before him, its form shimmering like a mirage in the desert heat. As he turned to face it fully, his heart stopped, his breath catching in his throat.

It was Odelia.

Her ghostly figure stood before him, her once vibrant eyes now hollow and haunting. The silky dress she wore spread around her like a web around a spider and the thin veil that draped her face only served to heighten the otherwordly aura that emanated from her being. It struck him that she always appeared like this, almost frozen in time.

John's mind was in turmoil, a aswirling vortex of conflicting emotions. Grief washed over him like a tidal wave, threatening to drown him in its depths. Love tugged at his heartstrings, a reminder of the bond he had shared with his late wife. And terror gripped him, knowing the power in the house would claim them all. He couldn't tear his eyes away from her, each detail etched into his memory from their life together. A bittersweet montage played out before him, a slideshow of cherished moments and painful reminders of all that was now lost.

"Odelia," he breathed, his voice barely above a whisper. "Here? Really"

The ghost tilted her head, a small, sad smile playing at the corners of her lips. "Hello, darling," she said, her voice echoing through the room like a siren's song.

John stood transfixed, his heart aching with a profound longing and despair. The sight of Odelia, even in her spectral form, stirred up everything threatening to consume him. He yearned to reach out, to touch her, to feel the warmth of her skin against his own once more, but he knew it would only lead to more pain

"John, my love," Odelia spoke, her voice sad and understanding. "You have to let me go. Vivienne needs you."

At the mention of Vivienne's name, John's heart clenched, torn between the love he held he still held for Odelia and the growing affection he felt for the woman who had stood by his side through his darkest hours. He closed his eyes, brow furrowed in anguish as he struggled to find the words to say.

"I... I don't know if I can, every time you appear I fear I cannot do it. Who looks after you now, in what there is for you?" He whispered, his voice raw.

Odelia's form drifted closer, her presence filling the room with melancholic serenity. "If you walk away from her, out of fear, out of some misguided idea it would be disloyal to me, I will haunt you into an early grave." John knew better than to think she wouldn't do it. "You're good for her and she's good for you. She challenges you... provokes you in the most delicious way. I like that. I like her."

John's interior raced, a jumbled mess, much like his exterior. Odelia's words echoed in his mind, strking a nerve he couldn't ignore. He knew she was right - he couldn't constantly be tempted to fall into a state of guilt and grief when alone. But the thought of releasing those emotions entirely felt indescribably scary. Could he do that without losing all that made him the man he was? His heart pounded in his chest as he grappled with the complexity of the decision ahead of him.

As Odelia's ghostly presence drew closer to John, her eyes filled with compassion, she gently touched his face, her ethereal touch sending shivers down his spine. The sensation was both familiar and foreign, a bittersweet moment and a reminder of the insurmountable barrier that now separated them. He was right. It was too painful.

"John, my love," Odelia whispered, "just let me go. You do me no kindness by keeping me here."

"What is it like, death?" He asked, hoping he could reassure himself.

"No, no, don't trouble yourself with that. You don't need to know." Odelia's voice hardened as she sought to be firm.

"Why won't you tell me?"

"None would tell you. Ghosts will not tell you what lies beyond death because they understand what they have lost. They will not encourage you to yearn for your grave and let the exquisite slices of heaven here on Earth pass you by. That slice." She pointed to the next room, and he understood her meaning all too well, hearing Vivienne scream through the door.

Planting one last kiss on his forehead, she backed away, leaving John to decide his path.

With her back straight and chin held high, Vivienne stepped forward to meet the towering beast. Her eyes glinted with determination and defiance as she faced it head-on. The air prickled with tension as she refused to back down. Fierce energy radiated from her as she spoke, her clear voice cutting through the chaos of the raging battle in the cottage.

"You have no power here," she declared, her words laced with an authority that seemed to emanate from the very depths of her being. "I will not be consumed by this house. I am stronger than any force you can muster. You have lost."

The creature's piercing eyes narrowed, the once fuller pupils mere sliers as they glinted with a menacing light. Its scaly body seemed to pulsate with an otherworldly energy, its darkened skin glistening in the light. Yet, despite it formidable appearance, the beast seemed to hesitate and shrink back at the unwavering stance of Vivienne. She stood tall, her jaw set in determination, radiating an aura of fearless defiance that seemed to give even the fearsome creature reason to pause.

With a crowbar in hand, John had forcefully pried open the old, battered door, causing splinters of wood to fly in all directions - and now watched the exchange with his heart in his mouth, fearful of Vivienne's safety.

Vivienne's voice cut through the fog like a blade, her words harsher toward the changeling than John had thought possible. "You have no power here. Your reign of terror ends now. Release your hold on this cottage and its lives, or face the consequences of your defiance."

Its towering body, casting an ominous shadow across the room, recoiled slightly at Vivienne's audacious proclamation. Its form, once gleaming with malicious intent, now flickered with a hint of uncertainty and even love, as if it had never encountered a mortal with such unyielding resolve. Any concern

John had that this creature would exploit her soft nature had long gone.

As the Demon's presence wavered, Vivienne pressed forward, her voice rising with each word. "I know what you are, I know why you are here! You live by my rules, or you face the consequences."

John strode across the floor with a determined gait, taking his place behind her. He stood tall and strong, guarding her from the wild wind that whipped through the room, sending objects flying in all directions. The force of the wind was like a hurricane, threatening to tear everything in its path apart. But John's presence provided a sense of safety and protection against the raging around them. Together they stood, braving the storm as a united force.

As the house's voilent outburst began to recede, its walls and furniture slowly fading back into their mundane forms, John stepped forward. His hand stretched out instinctively, seeking the comfort and stability of Vivienne's touch.

And in the quiet that followed, as the cottage seemed to exhale a long sigh of relief, John pulled her towards him. She melted into his embrace, feeling the warmth of his body against hers as he held her tightly. With one hand on her back and the other cradling her head, he pressed a gentle kiss onto the top of her head. They stood in each other's arms, their breathing slowly syncing until it was steady and calm in their chests.

The creature's eyes, once burning with malevolent intensity, now softened with understanding. It looked almost sad -

its body, shrouded in black scales and crowned with horns, diminishing, its face shining with tears, its growls tempered by wrenching sobs. Vivienne, feeling a compulsion, reached out as if to comfort it, but it backed away from her touch like a frightened animal. Slowly, as if acknowledging the greater power, it began to retreat, its presence fading like a shadow before the breaking dawn.

As the beast, now tamed, skulked away, Vivienne turned to John, her eyes pooling with tears. "It's over," she whispered, her voice trembling.

They stood in the blossoming light, still embracing, and felt the air lift around them. The house, seemingly resting, looked different in the natural light, still in need of care but mundane and human. Like torchlight to the underbelly of a bed, it had dispelled its monsters most ably.

What happened next was entirely up to them.

CHAPTER 27

Vampires Welcome at This Door

Now, dear reader, with all I had witnessed, I understood most certainly I had been wrong. Humanity was not the death of joy at all. Humanity was its one loyal soldier. Their story had been the end of the beginning and would be the beginning until it wasn't. Pain, like joy before it, would always end.

Sat atop the cold, sand-covered wall, I observed the quiet contentment of Vivienne and John, strolling along the beach hand-in-hand. The lovers, costumed in breezy linen, their faces a map of experience, revealed the depths of human connection that only itself could reveal. They laughed openly, their song carrying like the smell of salt on the air, as others paid no heed, their attentions focused on their own loved ones.

My yellowed eyes followed them as they descended into the free storm of the sea, a final victory over me. My crackled growl, with all the authority of the world beyond, carried on the wind like a command from beyond the veil, beseeching Death might venture forth. Yet, I troubled them little. Where once they looked upon my blackened, grungy scales, sleek horns, and cat-like eyes with fear and disgust, there was now a soft, almost pitying look as if they perceived my fallen status.

As long as I respected their boundaries, and didn't take up too much space, they were content to co-exist with me - a generosity I did not deserve. Never more than a solitary step behind, they would have been within their rights to be difficult about my presence, spending every conscious minute persecuting me into a temporary death. And while I would have relished such a fight, even craved it, they had extinguished the conflict without even a whimper. They had much more important achievements in mind.

My forked tongue, once searching out the salty tang of human grief, found no taste remained in it. How tragic, I mused, that it had taken such a humbling defeat to rehabilitate me.

I jumped up, the sand rippling away from me, and committed to giving this mortal humanity thing a try. In the distance, the first dimming of dusk crept in over us, rekindling the stars' fires, and death continued, unabated, unyielding, and ever-changing.

Vivienne and John looked back curiously, each offering their hand. Placing my clumsy hands in theirs, they embraced me as a parent embraced a child, their warm bodies feeling alien to my characteristically cold, dead skin.

I knew the significance of this moment would have echoes down the ages. Just as yours will.

Because the characters will change, and the setting will shift, but the story will remain the same.

And me? I will be waiting.

In the shadows, watching.

Until the end of time itself. Because that is how long your story remains.

NARRATOR'S NOTE CHALLENGE

There are a number of clues scattered throughout the Narrator's Notes. If you can figure out the answer, you can win a limited edition copy of the novel!

Pop your solution to the puzzle, a single sentence, to contact@igrainegray.co.uk - good luck.

Your Notes: